His Rock Hard Rhythm

Flora Dare, Josie Kell

DESCRIPTION

Alexis's middling witch powers? A grave disappointment to her parents.

The years of hard work? About to pay off!

Her gig of a lifetime? Managing one of the biggest orc rock bands in the world, Axebender.

The fly in the potion? The lead singer, Mace.

Their first meeting? He mistakes her for a groupie.

Now? It's showtime and Alexis has to prove she's not afraid of a pair of wicked tusks or deep green, totally lickable muscles that go on for days.

Copyright © 2022 by Flora Dare and Josie Kell

All rights reserved.

No portion of this book may be reproduced in any form without written permission from the publisher or author, except as permitted by U.S. copyright law.

Cover designed by MiblArt.

Contents

Dedication		VIII
1.	Chapter One	1
2.	Chapter Two	7
3.	Chapter Three	13
4.	Chapter Four	19
5.	Chapter Five	23
6.	Chapter Six	29
7.	Chapter Seven	33
8.	Chapter Eight	39
9.	Chapter Nine	45
10.	Chapter Ten	51
11.	Chapter Eleven	57
12.	Chapter Twelve	65

13.	Chapter Thirteen	71
14.	Chapter Fourteen	77
15.	Chapter Fifteen	81
16.	Chapter Sixteen	87
17.	Chapter Seventeen	93
18.	Chapter Eighteen	99
19.	Chapter Nineteen	105
20.	Chapter Twenty	113
21.	Chapter Twenty-One	119
22.	Chapter Twenty-Two	123
23.	Chapter Twenty-Three	127
24.	Chapter Twenty-Four	133
25.	Chapter Twenty-Five	139
26.	Chapter Twenty-Six	145
27.	Chapter Twenty-Seven	151
28.	Chapter Twenty-Eight	155
29.	Chapter Twenty-Nine	159
30.	Chapter Thirty	165
31.	Chapter Thirty-One	171
32.	Chapter Thirty-Two	177
33.	Chapter Thirty-Three	181
34.	Chapter Thirty-Four	185

35. Chapter Thirty-Five — 191
36. Chapter Thirty-Six — 195
37. Chapter Thirty-Seven — 201
38. Chapter Thirty-Eight — 207
39. Chapter Thirty-Nine — 211
40. Chapter Forty — 217
41. Chapter Forty-One — 221
42. Chapter Forty-Two — 227
43. Chapter Forty-Three — 233
44. Chapter Forty-Four — 239
45. Chapter Forty-Five — 243
46. Chapter Forty-Six — 249
47. Chapter Forty-Seven — 261
48. Chapter Forty-Eight: Epilogue — 267

About Authors — 273

Also By Flora Dare — 274

Special thanks to Marina Maddix and Ruby Dixon for helping whip these bad orcs of rock into shape and Celia Kyle for keeping our noses to the grindstone.

Chapter One

ALEXIS

"I mean, it's a promotion, that's a good thing," I said, as much to myself as to Shawna. "I mean, I should be really glad. I am glad. Of course I'm glad." I know I was babbling, but after everything that had happened with my last assignment, I could feel the anxiety welling up inside me.

Shawna Withern, who was supposed to be helping me pack, took an armload of clothes out of my suitcase and dropped it all onto my bureau. "Glad?" she squealed. "Alexis Marie Travers, you should be over the moon! This is huge! AxeBender is the absolute *best*."

"The best Orc Rock, maybe," I muttered, taking the clothes off the bureau and returning them to the suitcase.

"Yes, well, the worst Orc Rock is a move up from a stupid boyband!"

"Never Stop wasn't stupid. They were just—young. And pop-y."

But she wasn't wrong. Tour management for an actual high-profile rock band was definitely a move up from steering five teenagers past screaming tweens all day. Not to mention the way the whole thing ended.

Shawna started taking clothes out of my suitcase again. I took a beige linen shift dress out of her hands. "Why are you unpacking me?!"

I stared at the pile of clothes she'd moved, mustering up my magic to get it to fly back to the suitcase, but it wobbled like a pile of jello. The sleeve of a blouse fluttered like it was waving at me.

I gave up, and hoped Shawna hadn't noticed. Since she kept talking, it seemed like I'd dodged that bullet. Failing at magic triggered my anxiety and failing in front of someone? It felt a little bit like part of me dying. I could practically hear my parents scoffing at me. Before I fell too deep into that particular rabbit hole, I realized Shawna was shaking a lovely lilac-colored pantsuit at me.

"Because you can't wear any of this stuff on the new gig! It makes you look like someone's mom. Which totally made sense, when you were telling kids what to do." She chucked the pantsuit across the room, as far away from us as she could. She then rubbed her hands like she'd been touching something particularly icky.

I tried to protest, "Hey! My mom bought me that—" I stopped, realizing I'd basically proven her point. But Shawna wasn't done with me.

"The members of AxeBender will not take you seriously if you look like a frump. Neither will the venues. Or the hotels. No one. You will look completely out of place."

I stopped and stared at the boxy, pastel-pink pantsuit in my hands. She had a point. I groaned. "So what do I wear?" The way her eyes lit up, I knew she'd been waiting for the question.

"Wait here." She rushed into my large walk-in closet. A moment later she returned, carrying the clothes I saved for special occasions and dates. Not that I'd had many dates lately, or special occasions either. I turned my mind from that, ignoring how dusty some of the outfits were, and concentrated on how inappropriate for work they seemed.

"Seriously?" I held up a spangly silver top. "You think people will take me more seriously in this than if I wear mom clothes?"

Shawna glared at me, and I turned away. Shawna was my assistant, but she had a glare that could knock me over. I knew she wasn't really angry, but I still didn't like to be hit with it.

"You don't wear this top alone. You pair it with"—she picked up one of my favorite suit jackets—"this incredibly boring jacket, and a little black miniskirt. Together, they make an outfit for someone working in rock-and-roll. Get it?"

I didn't want to, but I had to admit it would be a pretty slamming look. Way better than my vast sea of pastel pantsuits. "All right, Shawna, I give in. Pack for me if you must."

She smiled triumphantly at me, perched at the edge of a chair and began to pick through the pile of clothes, matching things together as she went. It was nice to see her happy, even if the idea of changing my look so completely scared the hell out of me.

The pastels were leftovers from my parents' influence, gifts every year for Solstice in the hopes that I'd come to my senses and drop my rock-and-roll nonsense. That I'd become a sensible, practical witch. A practical witch wearing prim, pale pantsuits blending into the background, content to sit in my sister's shadow.

I left Shawna to it and picked up the giant envelope we'd been sent. I flopped across the bed, lying on my stomach and kicking my feet into the air. Inside the envelope I found a super-slick folder with our company's logo emblazoned on it in giant shimmering letters. *Totally subtle.* I opened it to read the information packet on AxeBender.

I already knew a little bit about them. They were the biggest Orc Rock band around at the moment, and you'd have to be living under a rock to have not heard about their antics. They trashed hotel rooms, threw raucous parties, smashed instruments—I groaned, and said again to Shawna, "It's a promotion, right? Not a punishment?"

I rifled through the pages and a picture of the band performing slid out a little. Goddamn, the lead singer was smoking hot. He was howling into a mic, sweat gleaming off his killer abs, and my mouth went dry. It should be illegal to be that unsettlingly hot.

"This lead singer, Mace—they're definitely not punishing me by making me work with a guy like this?"

"'A guy like this'?" Shawna raised her eyebrows at me. "What do you have against orcs, anyway?"

I gasped, horrified by the implications. "I've got nothing against orcs! It's not that I don't want to work with orcs, it's that I don't want to work with an alpha-hole who once bit a huge chunk out of a guitar and ate it, onstage!"

Shawna smirked. "I'm pretty sure that's a myth."

"It's not!" I waved a piece of paper from the folder at her. "He really did it! The rhythm guitarist was supposed to bring out a prop guitar, but he couldn't find it, so Mace did it with a real guitar instead! He cracked a tusk on it!"

Shawna laughed at me and picked up a skirt that was definitely way too short for business and added it to the Go pile. *Yikes.*

"Well that means he's devoted to his art! He doesn't let little mishaps get in the way of the show. And once you're in charge, the prop guitars will be where they're supposed to be."

I raised an eyebrow at her. "I'm not a stagehand."

"No, you tell the stagehands what to do."

I wanted to remind her that there were layers of people between me and the roadies, but she was right—the buck did stop with me. She stopped packing and sat down on the bed next to me. "You can do this, Alexis. You can more than do this. I've always known what you were capable of, and now—finally—the big bosses do too."

I smiled ruefully. "I suppose I should be glad about the whole horrible 'incident'?"

"No, you should be glad that when there was almost a horrific tragedy, you were there to save the day. I know I am."

The truth was, I'd surprised even myself at how well I'd handled that disaster. For once, my mind and my (usually pretty weak) magic had worked together seamlessly.

"Besides," Shawna continued, "Why did you become a tour manager in the first place? Was it because you wanted an easy job?"

I smiled at her. As she well knew, I'd started out as a publicist at the record label and transitioned to assisting a tour manager after confessing to my boss that I was starting to find my job monotonous.

My boss had been right—tour management was perfect for me. But I hadn't been experienced enough to take on a major band, and so had been assigned to an up-and-coming boy band. Which was fun, but different than what I'd imagined. What I'd imagined was excitement. And AxeBender definitely offered that, unlike the pre-pubescent pop scene of Never Stop.

"You're right," I told Shawna, and stood. "Everything's ready? Then we should get going. We're meeting them right after the show. I've got the backstage passes you've been craving."

Shawna looked me up and down, then laughed in my face. "You are not," she said flatly, "wearing *that* to a concert."

Chapter Two

ALEXIS

A few hours later, I stood in the wings at the AxeBender concert, waiting for it to start and wishing I'd been a little better at standing up to Shawna. The sequined minidress she'd insisted I borrow, then stuffed me into, wasn't quite as short on me as it would have been on her, but it still hit well above the knees. I glanced down at my cleavage and tugged the top up, as it did nothing to hide the chest I usually kept well-covered.

The strappy sandals I'd bought three years ago for a cousin's wedding had higher heels than I was used to and I worried I'd trip over something backstage and break my neck. *Note to self: Talk to Shawna about getting some sensible, badass combat boots like she wore.*

The long earrings she'd hung on me at the last minute brushed my neck every time I turned my head, sending weird shivers down my spine. My hair and make-up—well, she had a flair for it, and if I was being honest, I did feel pretty hot. But I wasn't used to looking so *fancy*. I looked way too fancy.

I leaned toward her, to whisper that I was going to go wash my face and try to brush my hair into something a bit more staid. But before I could, the stage lit up. The drummer hammered her kit and the guitarists started playing. Mace stepped up to the mic, opened his mouth and began to sing, and I forgot everything.

I forgot what I was wearing.

I forgot I hated my sister.

I forgot that my last relationship had turned out to be a catfish situation.

I forgot myself.

I was totally unprepared for what happened when Mace sang that first note, his body bending towards the fans.

I had been to concerts before, of course. Dozens, maybe hundreds. But never for an Orc Rock band. What little Orc Rock I'd heard had been mostly snippets—on the radio before I changed the station, or coming from Shawna's office before I texted her to turn it down. I had heard whole songs, of course, once or twice at the label offices, but I'd listened to them almost clinically. I'd vaguely assumed they weren't my type of music.

Hearing them live was totally different. The music surrounded me and got inside of me until my body was a part of the music. I saw people dancing below the stage and half wished I could join them, even though I'd always been baffled by people who moved like they were fighting, not dancing.

I settled for tapping my foot, and swaying—it seemed unprofessional to do more than that. To react, to lose control. Keeping control was paramount, otherwise I'd embarrass myself.

Of course, Shawna was dancing full-out beside me, hair flying. I nudged her and whispered that she should either stand still or go dance with the crowd. I was being sarcastic, but she squeezed my hand, whispered, "See you later" and ran off. She was amongst the fighters/dancers a few moments later.

I turned my attention back to the band, trying to concentrate on the stage setup, the ways the musicians and singer interacted with one another, where the extra amps were kept, but it was really no use.

The music swirled around me and engulfed me and I gave into it—still not dancing, but enjoying it, the way it sounded and the way it made me feel. Power flowed up my legs and into my body. The music made my heart sing and dammit, watching Mace belt out the song made my pussy clench as an unfamiliar warmth flooded between my legs.

Keep control, Alexis. You have to keep control.

Mace seemed to get even more energetic as the set went on, and I felt like he was pouring his energy into me. I was drinking him in, enraptured, tapping my feet and trying to keep from dancing, when he turned toward me and our eyes met.

It was like an electric shock.

I had never seen power like that, never felt that kind of intensity or passion. Something that wasn't quite human and wasn't quite animalistic but was somehow both and something more as well.

Of course, I'd known orcs my whole life. They were regular people, neighbors and classmates. I'd heard about rampaging, the way orcs could lose themselves to a sort of berserk bloodlust, like their ancestors had done eons before when going into battle. I'd certainly never seen it happen, though. Occasionally I saw someone come close to losing himself when playing sports or whatever, but they weren't actually out of control. This was different, this was so much more, this was truly an orc on a rampage, the kind you read about in descriptions of old wars.

This orc was rampaging with music, not violence, but it was a berserk rampage nonetheless. Trapped by his sky-blue eyes in a fiery gaze, I felt like prey but also like a predator. I wanted to join this rampage. I needed to be a part of it.

He turned back towards the audience and the effect lessened, though it didn't go away all together. I gradually became aware that my tapping feet were no longer tapping the floor, and I looked down to see that I was floating six inches in the air. I instantly fell back to earth, landing with a thud but staying upright thank goodness.

I pulled myself together, got myself under control and looked around hastily. Thank Luna that no one seemed to have noticed. Not that it would have mattered all that much, really. People knew some witches can fly, and while I didn't usually volunteer the fact that I was a witch, I also didn't really try to hide it, either.

But I didn't generally fly. I'd rarely had that kind of power. Not unless my tween charges were in mortal danger.

My sister flew all the time, of course, and a lot higher than half a foot off the ground. She did a lot of things I couldn't do. To hear my parents and most of the world speak, she was basically a modern-day goddess.

While she saved the world, I mostly made repairs in clothing, fixed up small wounds, moved things around a little if I was feeling really strong. Basically, my witch powers could be replaced by the kind of mini-emergency kit you stick in the side pocket of a suitcase. And my parents never, ever let me forget that.

I kept my feet firmly planted on the ground during the next few songs, and avoided eye contact with Mace. I still managed to enjoy the music way more than I'd ever have expected to. I couldn't help but feel a little disconcerted and more than a little hot and bothered. Relief flowed through my veins when the first set ended.

I gave the band time to get to their dressing rooms, not wanting to bump into them until I pulled myself together. So I wandered around a bit backstage until I found a ladies' room.

Inside, I cast one of my most useful spells, a quick 'stay' cantrip, so my makeup wouldn't budge, then splashed water on my face. I tried to remind myself that I was here to work. I leaned against the wall and wondered why I'd been able to fly. Okay, so I only floated. Close enough.

I tried not to think about how it felt to look in that orc's eyes, but failed. The memory of his gaze burning into mine made my body tingle again in a way that was unfamiliar but not altogether unpleasant.

Shawna sauntered in a bit later. She looked flushed and happy, and somehow wasn't sweaty at all, which seemed impossible.

"Shawna," I said, "why didn't you ever tell me how good this band is?"

She rolled her eyes so hard I thought they might get stuck. "I've been trying to get you to listen to Orc Rock—including this band—for as long as I've known you."

As we left the ladies room we could hear the band starting their second set. It wasn't as intense an experience this far away, but it still made my heart race with delight and I grinned at her. "Well, I should have listened. And, now," I glanced down at my watch, "we should get to the green room. The soon-to-be former tour manager told us to meet him there at eleven."

Chapter Three

ALEXIS

The green room looked exactly like every other green room I'd ever been in—lots of couches and chairs and tables of food and water. As we walked in, a portly man in his forties hurried towards us.

"Sorry," he said, "No one can be back here. At least right now. Try again after the show." He smiled unctuously and gave us both the slow up-down with his eyes.

My skin crawled and I set my teeth. I fake-smiled at him. "We're not fans, I'm Alexis Travers and this is my assistant, Shawna Withern. I'm the new tour manager."

His eyes widened a bit and he stopped leering. "Oh, it's so nice to meet you! I'm Horace, I was the tour manager until tonight." He took my hand into his damp, clammy one and shook it enthusiastically. "Sorry about that, I thought you were groupies—Well, we get a lot of fans coming backstage. I won't miss that part of the job."

He was clearly lying or he wouldn't have been eye-banging us with such vigor.

"I understand. We were with Never Stop before this tour. We had girls dressing like custodians, trying to get to the boys. Which was especially disturbing considering how many of the girls were twelve-year-olds."

He belched out something like a laugh and a wince combined. "I can only imagine. I'm glad I'll be leaving the band in good hands. Good work with that whole crazy incident."

I ignored his reference to the traumatic fiasco that had landed Shawna and me our new gig.

Shawna rolled her eyes at me behind his back and asked, as dry as a martini, "So, what's next for you, since you're leaving mid-tour?"

His false smile dropped a hair and he shrugged, "Family emergency. Unavoidable. I'm sure I'll be on the road again soon enough."

He led us into the room and we both grabbed bottles of water before sitting down at a table in the corner that he'd spread with paperwork.

He sat on the edge of his chair and glanced around the room constantly. I began to suspect he was a shapeshifter—antelope, maybe, or beaver. Definitely an herbivore. Total anxious prey vibe.

He took us through the tour schedule, which I'd already familiarized myself with, telling me which stops had problematic arena staff and which hotels had already canceled and needed to be rebooked. I was startled to see just how many hotels had decided that AxeBender was persona non grata.

"Of course there's always the tour bus, which has bunks to sleep in, but that's a last resort unless you're driving overnight." He peered at me. "I guess a bus will be an interesting change from planes, though, huh?"

I smiled and nodded. "Boy bands do not travel by bus unless it's for shuttling them between the airport and the venue and then the venue to the hotel. There's too much opportunity for under-age antics. We were planes all the way. I'm not saying I've sworn off air travel forever, but, well, I think I'll enjoy being on the ground for a while."

We continued going over tour plans for the next hour, AxeBender's performance faint in the distance. It was, as I expected, going to be a lot like managing any tour, as far as logistics went. The difficulty was going to be in keeping the band members under control, and convincing the venues and hotels to put up with their behavior.

Luckily I had my ace in the hole with Shawna. She could charm the hardest of ogres into giving her what she wanted.

The last encore played as we sat there chatting. The doors flung open and the green room began filling up. At first it was reporters, friends of the band, and some fans who'd sweet-talked their way in. Humans, orcs, shifters and supernatural creatures of all sorts milled around, slamming drinks and flirting.

Then silence as the band strutted through the door. Everyone started clapping as they filed in.

First up, the drummer, Freya better known as Frey, also the only girl in the band. She was as tall as the other orcs, but lithe and graceful, although more in the way a person swinging a broadsword might be called graceful. She was an emerald green stunner and looked dangerous as hell.

Next came Torch (real name, I had learned, Dennis), the lead guitarist. His jagged hair was dyed a vivid blue, in a shade that did not go well at all with his greenish skin, and he flashed a tight-tusked smile at the room.

Then the twins, Clash (Joe) and Jax (Jackson) walked in—no, they didn't walk, they *bounced*. They looked like gigantic puppies, beaming around the room, sweaty and smiling. A group of girls immediately rushed them, and they received them so warmly I worried panties might start dropping right then and there.

And then, a moment later, a few steps behind, came the lead singer. Mace (short for Mason) was taller than the others, and a little bit better built. He had bright blue eyes, unusual for an orc, and chiseled features. He entered the room like not only did he own it, but had conquered it and beat it into submission.

My heart skipped a beat.

He stopped, looked around the room, then threw his arms up and roared. The room roared back. I almost did too, but caught myself in time. That would not be proper for a tour manager. I'd already skirted the line of professionalism by losing myself so completely in the music that I'd floated. Me? Floating? I needed to keep a tight handle on myself.

Shawna did not have any such reservations. I'd encouraged her to take my old position as Never Stop's manager when it was offered, but watching her roar made me think that maybe she was right to turn it down. She was way more at home with Orc Rock than I was.

The only reason she'd passed on her own promotion, she said, was because she couldn't resist touring with AxeBender. I'd been glad, and guilty for being glad, to have her with me.

Chapter Four

ALEXIS

Someone turned on a sound system, and music filled the room—more Orc Rock—a band I didn't recognize (not surprising) but liked (surprising). I half kicked myself for never giving Orc Rock a chance. Especially now that I'd seen it live, where raw, authentic passion stopped me in my tracks and gave me no option but to be at one with the music.

The room took on a party atmosphere. The music wasn't so loud that you had to shout to be heard, but Horace leaned a little too close towards us anyway before he spoke. "I'll introduce you to the band members, but, um, not just yet." I followed his eyes to the band, standing together and toasting, and understood that they needed a moment to come down from the show. "But soon," he added, and as I saw how much they were drinking, and how quickly, I understood that, too.

Horace swept the papers up off the table and Shawna took them off his hands. She tucked them back into a folder, stuck them efficiently piled up on the table in front of me, winked, and hustled off to get a drink. Right next to where Torch was being served, I noticed.

I, personally, don't like to drink on the job but Shawna can hold her liquor like no one I've ever seen. She can throw back shots of whiskey all night and never stumble or slur her words.

Truthfully, I'm kind of a lightweight when it comes to booze and there is no way I'd be able to keep it together if I had more than one weak drink. It wasn't a big deal when we were working with Never Stop, but now I might need to start drinking tonic with a twist of lime so it looked like I was imbibing.

My stomach grumbled loudly, and I realized I was absolutely starving. The perils of skipping dinner to let Shawna give me a glow-up. I moved toward the big buffet table heaped with all sorts of food—steak and lobster at one end, cookies and pastries at the other. I went simple and fast and grabbed a bagel off the middle of the table. I was spreading cream cheese on it when someone came up next to me.

I could feel a sort of heat and power radiating off of whoever stepped behind me. I turned, knowing it had to be Mace, his big dick energy coming off him in waves. I told myself the sudden drool I was struggling to control was entirely due to my bagel and not the personification of a smoking hot rock god standing next to me.

His human-sized tee-shirt was ragged, the sleeves cut off and slits cut in the sides to make it fit his massive torso. I tried to feel snarky about it, knowing for a fact that they made that exact tee-shirt in orc sizes, but the truth was I didn't mind being able to see his rippled muscles, not at all. I tore my eyes away, willing myself to look only at his face, and trying to ignore the scent of him, which quickly drowned out the odors of the food.

He smelled—good. Very good. Distractingly good. Like leather and musk and a little bit of wild forest.

As I watched his face, from the way his bright blue eyes wrinkled and the way his tusks curved up from his full lips, I forgot to hold onto the knife. For once my magic worked well and it continued to spread cream cheese neatly onto the bagel. Neat was not usually in my wheelhouse, so that was nice.

His tusks were big. Really big. Was it true what they said about the size of a guy's tusks matching the size of his cock? I then stopped thinking that way immediately, as I was a professional and what the hell. So I didn't think about how big his cock might be, but I kept looking at his tusks. His big, thick tusks. My heart sped up and my panties grew damp.

Way to keep it professional.

He glanced down at me, smiled and winked, then turned back to the table, reaching for horseradish sauce to put on the plate of beef he was holding.

The music had quieted a bit as the party had spread to other, larger areas, and I figured it was as good a time as any to introduce myself.

"Hi!" I said, quickly grabbing the floating knife and plate, then putting them down so I could shake hands. "I'm your—"

I was going to say "new tour manager," but I didn't get to finish. He glanced at me again, smiled even wider, and said "Autographs and blowjobs later, sweet cheeks. I've gotta eat." Then he turned his back on me and walked away.

I considered flinging my knife into his back.

Instead, I grabbed Shawna and marched back over to Horace.

"We should probably get our passes set up, before it gets too late." What I wanted to scream was we should have done it first thing and then maybe the lead singer of the band we were going to be touring with wouldn't have both rudely propositioned me while blowing me off.

"Oh, right, I forgot about that." Horace stumbled over to his briefcase and hauled it up onto the coffee table. Somehow, he'd managed to get three sheets to the wind. He belched and a sour stench wafted over Shawna and me. "Right, hands out." He slapped the all-access passes on our hands, then tapped them with glowing amethyst. A tingle swept from the crown of my head to the tip of my toes and I shivered as the magic scanned us. The pass glowed purple for a moment. "And that's that. You now have the highest level of access. Guess this is yours now too."

A tinge of bitterness laced his words as he tossed me the stone.

Chapter Five

MACE

I couldn't get away from her fast enough. I managed to saunter casually until I was out of the room, then darted into my empty dressing room and sat on the bench, balancing my plate on the table, wondering what the hell was wrong with me. I don't usually run away from groupies.

I don't run towards them either—at least not since our first tour when I gave Jax and Clash some real competition.. But I realized pretty fast that sex with groupies was literally fucking tedious. Making sex that boring should be a crime. It wasn't my thing.

But I wasn't scared of them, either. Usually when I met groupies I'd be charming and friendly and, as long as they were of age, I'd send them in the direction of the twins, who seemed determined to spread the ideals of sex positivity across the country one chick at a time. Sometimes three or four chicks at a time.

But then this woman came along and next thing I knew I was hiding, eating a sandwich in the near-dark.

When she'd been on the side of the stage, it had been okay. Groupies make it to the side of the stage sometimes, usually by sweet-talking a roadie who recognizes her as the type of girl someone in the band likes.

And I could barely make her out in the gloom, really, so it was no big deal. I mean, I knew she was there. I could *feel* her there. I could feel her taking the music I was feeding her. I could feel her taking it in and turning it into raw power and sending it back to me, making me more connected to the music than seemed real.

Okay, yes, it was a big deal when she was at the side of the stage. She absolutely rocked my mind and body from the moment our eyes met. One glance and I forgot the next line and had to throw it to the audience to fill in the lyrics for me.

But then she wasn't there for the second set and I was disappointed, like super disappointed, but also relieved because I didn't need that kind of distraction. The last thing I needed was to get twisted up with another disastrous road girlfriend.

And I definitely wasn't looking for a fling with a groupie.

Until I saw her in the green room and suddenly thought, maybe I was looking for exactly that. I moved in next to her, ready to introduce myself and convince her to sneak away with me. Oh man, the way she smelled was like nothing else, or maybe kind of like a spring meadow. Sunshine and flowers.

I could feel her energy jolting through me, pulling me towards her but then she spoke. And it was too much. It was a thousand times more powerful than I'd ever felt with Aubrey. I panicked.

I did not need this hassle, the hassle of being so into someone you lose yourself. So into someone that when they leave you, you have no idea who you are. I couldn't risk that again. Risk myself. Risk the band. Not again. *Never* again.

So I kept it cool and then I ran and hid. Like the grown-ass rock star I am. I ran like my shirt was on fire and found the closest hidey-hole to barricade myself in, terrified she could tell I was rock-hard for her, and I didn't even know her name.

I ate slowly and told myself I definitely wanted, no, *needed* her to leave before I left my hideaway. Or maybe she'd fuck someone else in the band, who could then tell me about it.

Or maybe I could find her and fuck her myself and tell *them* about it.

Or not tell them about it because I was busy fucking her some more, fucking her hard and deep, hearing her scream my name.

I shifted, my erection straining against the leather of my pants. Could I jerk off in the dressing room without someone walking in on me? What would happen if *she* walked in on me while I was jerking off? *Damn it, stop thinking about her.* About that sweet pout of a mouth and what it would look like if she slid down my body to her knees, looking up at me.

I leaned against the door and wrestled my pulsating cock out of my pants before it broke the zipper. I wrapped my hand around my thickness, and stroked from the root to the tip, squeezing a little harder as each ridge passed through my fingers. Precum slicked my hand, and I thrust the crown of my cock between my fingers. I thought about the way she smelled of sunshine and flowers, how it might feel to grab her by the waist and pull her against me—and came all over my hands.

I was still cleaning it up when my phone chimed. It was Frey.

Dude, you disappeared! I know you aren't banging anyone in the dressing room, so where the fuck are you? Did you forget? It's Asshat's last night and the new tour manager is here.

I groaned out loud. I'd been so focused on getting off that I'd forgotten about that. Good thing I'd taken care of myself before having to be all professional.

We'd pushed poor, terrible Horace way past the limits of his abilities, so it was a relief to have a new tour manager. Family emergency, my ass. He'd been hooking up with some chick, knocked her up and his wife was about to kick him out. She should, she deserves loyalty from her partner.

I made my way back to the green room and my heart started pounding the moment I walked in. There was the rest of the band. There was that useless creep Horace.

There was some girl I didn't recognize, but was oddly certain I wouldn't want to fight, and there—there was *her*. There she was. Looking at me coolly, with an expression that made it suddenly incredibly obvious that she was not a groupie at all. And all my dreams of her delicious, full lips stretched around my cock were way off the table.

Oh, sweet fuck. Fuck, fuck, fuck. Frey was going to absolutely murder me if she found out I'd already managed to insult what I guessed was someone really important.

"Mace, good, you're here," Horace said in that voice that made me want to shove him into a locker. "This is your new tour manager, Alexis."

I'm pretty sure I didn't let the shock and embarrassment and general horror show on my face. I mean, orcs are lucky that way—our faces aren't used to those expressions.

Chapter Six

MACE

Alexis held out her hand to me and I cautiously shook it. I was always careful about not crushing human hands. But now I was actually scared that if I touched her I might be overcome with lust, and do something incredibly foolish like throw her over my shoulder and kidnap her, like orcs in the olden days did when they found their mate.

But it didn't happen. I kept my shit together. She was still, easily, the most beautiful woman I'd ever seen and definitely the sexiest.

God, what kind of tour manager wears an outfit like that, anyway?

I mean, absolutely, women should wear whatever they want without being objectified—but who shows up in a green room looking better than the hottest groupie on earth and oozing sex vibes and expects everyone to assume they're the tour manager and not there to meet my deepest most carnal desires, to fulfill fantasies I hadn't even known I had.

I shook my head, trying to chase out the lustful thoughts. Touching her did not cause me to be overcome with desire. There was no spark like there'd been earlier on stage, no electricity pouring into me. I was shaking hands with a beautiful woman, but a beautiful woman who really didn't like me much.

Which wasn't surprising. I'd told our new tour manager I didn't have time to give her an autograph or get a blowjob. Oh god. Maybe if I *explained*, if I told her that I'd been trying really hard to not bend her over the buffet table?

No, that probably would not make things better.

Alexis dropped my hand and turned slightly away from me, addressing the band in general without ever meeting my eyes, telling us things about schedules and contract riders and how we should probably not trash hotel rooms, keeping our charms against pregnancy and disease well-charged, the usual stuff.

I zoned out, counting on my bandmates to catch me up on anything I really needed to know. Even acting all cold, even with any spark between us definitely gone forever, I still couldn't help but notice the way her breasts strained against the thin fabric of her dress.

Thank god my stiff leather pants disguised my erection. Because despite taking myself in hand earlier, I definitely had one again.

By the time everyone had finished talking I had gotten a hold of myself a bit. As we dispersed, preparing to go back to the hotel, I gently caught her elbow and pulled her aside. I had to make this right or my bandmates would rightfully string me up, no matter how fond of me they were.

"Listen," I said, my voice sounding a lot more gruff than usual. "I'm really sorry about earlier. I shouldn't have treated you like that. Hell, I don't usually treat actual groupies like that. I was a dick and nothing like it will ever happen again."

She smiled, sort of. That passionate, full, flirty mouth was now a hard, thin line. "Good," she said in an ice-cold voice. "I will enjoy being treated in a professional manner moving forward. I'm sure you're capable of that, if you try."

She tried to walk away, but I blocked her. "Look at it this way," I said, making my eyes as puppy-dog-like as an orc's eyes can be. "This is the most embarrassed I've been in years. The only thing worse would be if you told everyone about it. So you have that to hold over my head. How often does a tour manager have so much power over a performer? I'm going to be doing whatever you say as long as you keep this between us."

To my utter delight, warmth came into her eyes and she laughed, a melodic trill that would have sent shivers down my spine if I still felt that way about her which I did not—it was probably the air conditioning or something.

"That's a fair point," she said. "You humiliating yourself like that may have made my job a lot easier."

She smiled and walked away. I didn't watch her ass as she walked away so much as I just continued to look in that direction. It wasn't my fault her ass was where I happened to be looking.

Chapter Seven

MACE

Back at the hotel, my big plan had been to finish my book and maybe take a bath if the tub was big enough. Instead, I found myself pacing the room, unable to quiet down. I was still horny as hell and frustrated beyond measure.

When I heard the giggles in the hall that meant groupies had found our floor, I did something I hadn't done in years—I opened the door and beckoned them inside. But as soon as the three of them stood eagerly by the bed—no doubt wondering if the tusk size thing was true—I realized it was no good.

They were very pretty, and probably enjoyably flexible, but they weren't *her*. All I wanted was Alexis and drowning myself in random pussy would only make me feel depressed and lonely.

So I made up an elaborate story so they understood that it wasn't them it was me and they were definitely the hottest, coolest women I'd ever seen in my life. I ushered them back into the hall and gave them the twins' suite number, hoping they weren't at full capacity already.

After they'd left, hugging me goodbye very sweetly, I turned to go back into my room and found myself looking directly at Alexis. She was dressed in sweats and slippers, going into her room with a bucket of ice, and any warmth I had ever seen in her face was definitely gone.

Was it clear those groupies had left my room after NOT fucking me? If it wasn't clear, how could an orc casually bring that up? How could a woman possibly look that fuckable in sweats and slippers? Would it be okay to walk over, pull out my suddenly throbbing cock, and screw her up against the wall?

Before I could get the answers to any of those questions, she'd gone into her room. She didn't slam the door, but she didn't shut it softly either.

I went into my room and thought about shredding those damn sweats and exposing those sweet, luscious curves. I groaned and took myself in hand, thinking about her, *again*.

The next morning I woke up to cum-covered sheets for the first time since I was fifteen. I tried to remember the dream, but all I could bring back was the sound of Alexis's voice in my ear, and the feel of her hips against mine.

Thinking about actually touching her sent me to a cold shower, which didn't help at all and ended with me coming so hard the tile wall cracked a little. I'd heard other orcs claim they could do that, but had never seen it happen outside of porn. Turns out all it takes is a hot tour manager and me going absolutely insane.

I waited as long as I could before I headed downstairs to get on the tour bus. I wanted to see where she was sitting and sit as far away from her as possible. When I stepped on, I accidentally caught her eye and she smiled that ice-cold smile.

"Please try to be on time in the future," she said as I passed. "Staying on schedule is incredibly important."

"Absolutely boss, I will not be late again!" I tried to be incredibly charming but it clearly bounced right off her.

As I walked down the aisle to grab a seat in the very back, Frey whispered "Oooh you got in trouble!" and laughed when I gave her the finger.

The second my ass hit the cushion, my cell phone binged with a text. It was from Frey.

> *Do NOT fuck the tour manager. Do not be that stupid. She will fall for you and then she will hate you and then she will ruin the tour.*

I scowled and was real happy I was sitting in the back because there was a good chance I was blushing. Which was stupid because orcs don't blush. In fact, I'm pretty sure orcs can't physically blush. And yet, my face felt awfully hot. I texted her back:

> *Fuck you. I'm not stupid. Besides, she hates me already.*

I wondered if that was true, and hoped it wasn't. But deep down, I knew I'd definitely gotten on Alexis's bad side.

Bing.

> *She might hate you but you looked like you'd fuck her on the bus floor if she let you.*

I didn't respond and I was trying hard to not imagine fucking Alexis on the floor of the bus when another text came from Frey.

> *And as far as her hating you, you better fix whatever that's about before it messes up the tour. The record label isn't going to keep replacing managers and paying off hotels. We're not that good. Make her like you. Figure out a way to charm her.*

I finally typed back to Frey:

> *Fine, don't worry. I'll charm the pants off her.*

Then I took some deep breaths, wondered what the hell was wrong with me, and deleted the second sentence before hitting send.

With Frey mollified and the rest of the band snoozing, I stared out the window at the highway rushing by. Maybe it would be a good idea to fuck some groupies at the next stop after all. Maybe a whole lot of groupies.

Alexis' laugh floated to the back of the bus and I realized I desperately wanted to pull out all the stops to get back into her good graces. I would do anything in the world to hear that laugh as much as possible. Hearing her amusement made the sides of my lips upturn and put me in a much better mood. I glanced down the aisle and saw her checking some documents in front of her, then texting madly. Horace mostly slept off a hangover on the bus, rarely actually working in front of us.

I can do this, I told myself. I was an adult, and she was clearly an intelligent woman. I could think of her as something other than the sexiest creature—orc, human, or shifter—I'd ever laid eyes on. I could stop embarrassing myself in front of her, too.

I would treat her like a colleague, and I would be charming enough to make her like me. I mean, not like me that way, like me as a coworker whose tour she was managing. Sure, I might have to jerk off every hour or so, and maybe let off some steam by reminding myself what enthusiastic consent sounds like when it's screamed by a group of women eager to do all the work.

But I could do it.

I could stop thinking about what her lips would feel like crushed against mine, what her breasts would feel like under my hands, how sweet her pussy probably tasted—

God damn it. This was going to be a fucking long tour.

Chapter Eight

ALEXIS

Working on the tour bus was easier than I expected. The seats were extremely comfortable and even more spacious than first class on a plane. And best of all, there was a table I could monopolize. I had my laptop out and my papers spread out in front of me. I emailed the record label, verified venues, and authorized merch with ease.

Shawna sat across the row, talking to hotels, making sure the band would have places to stay. A lot of that ended up being on the phone, because most hotel managers wanted to actually hear the voice of the person promising that their precious rooms would remain untrashed.

It was nice to have my mind and hands occupied, so that I didn't have time to think about certain orcs who were not only incapable of telling the difference between a groupie and a tour manager, but were also apparently incapable of keeping their hands off the actual groupies.

Which was absolutely ridiculous for me to be upset about. He was a rock star. Part of the allure of being a rock star was being surrounded by beautiful and willing women. I knew I was being maybe a little bit irrational.

And I definitely didn't think about how he was ready to blow me off completely when he thought I was a fan, even though he clearly had nothing at all against *some* fans. Apparently I was not his type, which was obviously a good thing. Literally the last thing I needed in my life right now was some big, handsome, buff orc hitting on me.

Ugh, who would want that? Who would want a hateful, sex-obsessed rock god?

My mind drifted back to the dream I'd had the night before, the dream in which despite me not actually wanting him at all, Mace had been on top of me, thrusting, my legs wrapped around him, heels pounding his ass trying to drive him somehow even deeper inside of me—

Quickly, I turned my attention to the press pictures from last night. There was one that made me quiver with need, the lights hit Mace just so, highlighting his unbelievable arms as he howled into his mic. It took everything to pull myself together and actually focus on the tasks at hand.

I finally busted through all the important issues and distracted myself with busy work. I looked up when Shawna came bustling up, scooped all the papers from the table, and slid into the seat next to me. She unceremoniously stuffed them into a folder before handing me a soda she'd snagged from the fridge at the front of the bus.

"I'll feel guilty for taking a break unless you take a break too," she said.

I closed my laptop and opened the soda. "Well I wouldn't want you to feel guilty," I said, taking a swig. "How are the hotels?"

"Mostly sorted. Still have a few that might be a problem, but those aren't for a few weeks. But it'll work out. I did have to do a lot of talking, though." She glanced around to make sure we weren't overheard. "Between us girls, man, Horace sure wasn't great at his job."

"No, he really wasn't," I agreed. "Though from what the label told me, he was at his worst when it came to keeping the band in line." I glanced around too, to be doubly sure no one could hear us, but the band were all sitting towards the back of the bus playing some sort of card game that mostly seemed to involve elaborate orcish swearing. "We're going to have to make sure we don't have that problem. What do you think of them?"

Shawna smiled and shrugged. "Torch seems really funny and shockingly sweet. The twins are sort of—not dumb, exactly, but eager to please. Frey and I haven't talked much. I'm worried she might be one of those girls who has to act tough all the time and only hangs out with guys. I can't get a sense of Mace at all. You?"

I shrugged. "Same. Didn't seem like they caused any trouble in the rooms last night, from what I heard. Although they were definitely entertaining groupies. Some of them, anyway."

"Really?" Shawna's eyes widened and she leaned in, eager for a good gossip. "Who?"

"Mace, definitely. I saw some leaving his room." Keeping the snide tone out of my voice almost killed me. I had no right or reason to be jealous and snippy about it. But here I was, mad at a rock star for acting like a rock star. "And the yowls coming out of Jax and Clash's room made it sound like they had a dozen apiece."

"Not Torch though?" Shawna asked, "Oh, or Frey?"

"No idea," I shrugged. "Their rooms were down the hall. I didn't hear or see anything, but that doesn't mean much."

Shawna nodded. "Well, I guess as long as the fans are all of age and all of them want to be there, it's cool. We don't have to worry about tweeners, the way we did with Never Stop."

"Thank goodness for that," I laughed.

"How much longer till we get there, anyway?" Shawna asked, stretching. "And do we get to stop for lunch or anything?"

"There should be sandwiches in the fridge," I told her, "And the trip isn't long enough for a stop. We'll hit town in about thirty minutes."

"Won't that give us an awful lot of time before the show?"

"Yes, but we'll need it," I said. "You and I are going to have to visit every vendor, talk to every roadie, examine every setup, make sure the audio engineer is a happy camper. Anything goes wrong tonight, it's on us."

"But nothing will go wrong," Shawna said with a smile. "It's us!"

She was right, and everything went as smooth as butter. By the time the show ended, I was exhausted. Managing an orc rock band was about a thousand times more complicated than working with a prepubescent boy band.

For one thing, the members of the band were a whole lot more likely to have minds of their own about what was best, and threatening to call their parents wasn't really an option. Although they did seem awfully close to their families. Maybe calling their folks would actually work, if I got desperate enough.

CHAPTER NINE

ALEXIS

Before we left the venue for the hotel, I'd gathered the band together for a quick meeting.

"Alrighty, guys, so we're all super clear, like, absolutely *crystal clear*, you will not, I repeat, NOT mistreat the hotel staff. Also—I ticked each item off on my fingers—"you will not trash your rooms. There will be no flooding of bathrooms. Nor tossing food at room service."

Frey elbowed Jax who tried to look like an angel who'd never dare do such a thing. Clash grinned at me and Torch laughed, shaking his head at his bandmates' antics.

"No worries, boss lady," Torch said. "We're here for two nights. You don't throw a TV into a pool if you're going to want to swim the next day. Everybody knows that!"

I started to respond but they all began to wander away. I was going to let them until Mace winked at Jax and rolled his eyes.

My temper rose and so did the table next to me. I relaxed my power and it hit the floor with a loud thump that was almost a crash. The band all froze, slowly turned and stared at me.

"Look," I said, using the same voice I used when the boy band got out of hand. "This isn't a joke. We're having a very hard time getting hotels for you." I trapped Torch with my eyes. "If you don't keep your nose clean, you can sleep in the bunks on the bus. But you know as well as I do, that isn't comfortable or especially restorative. If you want to keep up your schedule, you need to show some goddamn restraint." Torch lowered his eyes to the floor.

My eyes swept to each band member, until they each dropped their gaze from mine. "Real adult talk. The record label isn't willing to put up with much more of this bullshit. You only make them so much money and they're not going to let the hotel bills eat up all the profit. If we can't get hotel rooms, at something well-under the "you might destroy us" rate, we can't tour. And if we don't tour, the record label is going to decide you're not worth it, and drop your asses before the next album. Got it?"

They all stared at me, shuffling their feet, speechless. Finally, Torch spoke again. "Got it," he muttered. He looked slightly embarrassed.

"But you know," Mace cut in, and I forced myself to look at him. Not wanting to meet his eye, I stared at his tusks, the way they curved up over his lip in a way that made me want to kiss him. I mean, not him, I thought it might be fun to make out with an orc sometime. Any orc. Just not Mace. With great effort, I concentrated on his words.

"It's not so much that we enjoy causing trouble as that our fans expect us to be, well, troublemakers. We have reputations as bad-asses, and they expect that. Every time we do something that pisses people off, it ends up in the paper and makes our fans like us more."

"Be that as it may," I said, annoyed because I knew he was right, "you still need to toe the line. Starting now. We can always do a set-up so you still look like bad-asses without jeopardizing your entire careers. Oh, and that reminds me—please make sure your charms against pregnancy and disease are recharged."

Rather than let Mace argue further, or let him be sexy at me, I turned and left. I couldn't wait to get to the hotel. I hoped my room had a good bathtub. I was going to need to soak away the tension from this meeting.

My room did, as it turned out, have a good bathtub. In fact, it had a simply enormous bathtub. Which fit nicely with the enormous bathroom. An enormous bathroom that was attached to an enormous bedroom connected to the rest of the enormous two-bedroom-plus-giant-living room suite I was sharing with Shawna.

"Okay, seriously, who did you blow to get a room like this? What did you do to get us this impossible suite," I asked her, staring around at the plush velvet furniture, the thick drapes, the huge pile of satin pillows on my king-sized bed.

Shawna smiled and shrugged. "We're going to be here for two nights, like Torch said. I figured you and I could use a little luxury."

"But how much of the budget did this eat up?" It wasn't that I was used to roach motels, but this place was beyond extravagant. I was pretty sure the rock-and-roll lifestyle did not lead to these kinds of opulent digs. Not until they were way, way, WAY more successful.

"None." Shawna looked a little bit sheepish. "The owner knows my parents, they went to school together, okay? No one happened to be staying in the presidential suite this week, so I was able to get us upgraded for free. I figured you deserved it, to celebrate the promotion and all."

I considered arguing, but decided instead to find out how well-stocked the bar in the corner was. To my delight, it was *very* well-stocked. To be polite I made Shawna a Cosmo before going to work making myself a complicated rum punch. The cliche is true: Witches are a sucker for super-fancy cocktails. Reminds us of brewing up a potion, I suppose.

Shawna lit a fire in the fireplace—this room was truly ridiculous—and we sat together on the velvet couch, stretching our feet towards the dancing flames.

I'd only taken one sip when there was a timid knock at the door.

Chapter Ten

ALEXIS

Frey stood in the doorway, looking slightly nervous. "Hi," she said. "You all aren't going to sleep yet, are you? I mean, if you are, that's fine, I can come back tomorrow. Or whenever."

"No, we're good," I said, opening the door wider and stepping aside to let her in. "Come in and warm up by the fire."

Frey's eyes widened as she entered the spacious suite. "Wow, this place is fancy!"

"Yeah, we're not used to it either. It's a surprise one-time perk." I didn't need her complaining that the tour manager's room was nicer than the talents' rooms, especially after I'd roundly scolded them. "Would you like a drink?" Then I cringed inside, because orcs don't drink the same booze as humans, and I hadn't thought to see if the hotel had stocked any orc drinks.

"Uh, yeah," she said, peering at the bar and spotting what I had missed. "I'll grab that bottle of creme de menthe and orxxstrax, if that's cool."

"We do have glasses," I said, walking over to the bar and grabbing the bottle with relief.

"Oh, no, that's okay. The bottle is fine."

Once again, I felt like an idiot. Of course I knew orcs had trouble drinking out of glasses that weren't specially designed for them. And at a quick glance, there weren't any of those at the bar. Maybe the hotel only bothered with additional glassware if orcs rented the room? That seemed like an oversight with such a fancy room. But at least they had stuff for orcs to drink.

I started to apologize but she laughed and took the bottle from my hand. "Don't worry about it, I like bottles anyway."

She took a hearty swig and sat down by the fire. She smiled at us, and seemed relaxed in a way I hadn't seen before, if still a little shy.

"Do you know," she said, "we almost never have women on tour with us, other than me? The managers are always dudes, our roadies have all been dudes, and of course the rest of the band is all dudes. And don't get me wrong, I love my dudes, but—"

Shawna cut in. "But you must go out of your fucking mind."

"I really, really do." Frey laughed. "I haven't had anyone to paint my toenails with in forever."

"Wait a sec," I said, "surely the guys sometimes bring girls on the bus? I guess they probably weren't there to paint their toenails with you, but at least they'd be some female company?"

"Not really," Frey said with a shrug. "Jax and Clash are the only ones who really spend time with groupies, and they like to find new ones in every town." She rolled her eyes. "They always treat the lady fans well, and they say part of that is not tricking them into thinking they're getting anything serious. Of course that works out well for them, too."

"But what about Torch? And, um, Mace?" I asked, remembering the bevy of blondes, brunettes, and emeralds leaving his room the night before.

She took another swig from the bottle and shook her head. "Torch has never slept with a groupie in his life, bless his heart. He had a super-serious girlfriend until last year, when she broke his heart." Frey swore under her breath. "I would have loved it if she'd toured with us, but she always stayed home. Turned out that was because she had another boyfriend she didn't want to take time away from."

"Oh no, poor Torch!!" Shawna looked horrified.

Frey nodded. "He's been nursing a broken heart ever since. Gotten a bit maudlin to tell you the truth." She shook her head. "And as for Mace—Well, he's kind of an idiot. He slept around on our first tour, like Jax and Clash. Then he'd have casual girlfriends, nothing especially long lasting. But then, last tour, he fell for someone. Her name was Aubrey, and she was a piece of fucking work." She scowled and took a long chug out of her bottle.

I took a sip of my drink and was barely able to keep the interest off my face.

"Fucking Aubrey. It was the one time we finally had another girl on our tour bus, and trust me, there was no interest in going shopping or getting pedicures together." Frey stared down at her hand and looked a little sad.

"She was the sort of girl who hates other girls. She was super jealous of me, and was certain I had something going with Mace which is hilarious and *gross*. We've known each other our whole lives." Frey made a face and shuddered. "It's hard to feel romantic about a guy who you once sat on and forced to eat a mud pie, you know?"

Shawna giggled and I tried to envision Mace pinned down and covered in mud, but that thought path got x-rated pretty quickly. Everything I thought about Mace got extra sexy, extra fast.

Frey continued. "But she was super jealous and possessive, always accusing him of looking at other girls, and insisting he do whatever she said, and whenever he tried to stand up to her, she cried. It was awful. But he was so far gone, there was nothing we could do. He was talking marriage, kids, everything."

"So what happened," I asked, leaning forward and forgetting to act casual.

Frey smiled bitterly and shrugged. "We played a festival. The headlining band was Orkestra," she said, naming the band that was definitely the biggest Orc Rock band in the country at the moment, maybe in the world. "Aubrey met a rock star a little more famous and a little more rich than Mace, and that was it. She was gone. The night he planned on asking her to marry him."

Frey took one last gulp from the bottle, emptying it. "It was super ugly. Mace raging on his knees in the rain, yelling at the Gods, *ugly*. We were trying to comfort him while also trying not to show how thrilled we were that Aubrey was gone."

She leaned back and looked sad and morose.

"Luckily the tour was almost over. His mom and my mom showed up, and he went to a resort somewhere to recover for a couple months. When came home, he refused to talk about it. He hasn't mentioned her name since. And he hasn't been with anyone, either. One thing I can tell you with absolute certainty: No groupies for Mace."

I thought again of the group of young women leaving his room, and shrugged. Maybe he'd started up again, getting back into the saddle. *Why did that sting so bad? Who knows.*

"And how about you, Frey," Shawna asked teasingly. "Do you run around with groupies?"

"Why yes, yes I do," Frey said with a delighted grin. "But we are definitely not painting toenails together. I enjoy throwing—let's call them group gatherings—for men and women who, ahhh, like naked group gatherings."

I grinned at her turn of phrase, a very polite way of saying she organized raucous orgies. "I always forget there are male groupies too."

"Oh trust me, there are," Frey laughed. "I bet at least a few of them would have a thing for hot tour managers, if you'd like me to send some over."

"Don't you dare," I said, while Shawna hooted with glee.

I finished my drink and made another, and the conversation turned to favorite movies and cutest actors and what famous people we'd met. It was a nice evening and when Frey left, she hugged us both. "This was so much fun," she said. "I'm so glad you guys are here."

It made me feel glad too. If nothing else, I had a friend in Frey.

Shawna went off to take a bath—her bathroom's tub was as gigantic as mine—and I decided that even better than a soak would be a swim. I slipped into my suit, grabbed a couple towels and headed to the pool. I prayed I'd be able to burn off enough energy that I could keep Mace out of my head.

CHAPTER ELEVEN

ALEXIS

Night swimming in hotel pools has always been my way of relaxing on tours. This pool was nicer than most, heated and shaded with palm trees. I thought they were probably fake, but they looked real enough to be charming. Plus they hid the pool from view enough that for half a heartbeat I considered skinny-dipping.

As soon as I slipped into the warm water, the tension that had been coiled in my back and neck began to melt away. I swam a few lazy laps, then floated on my back, staring up at the twinkling stars through the palm fronds. The water lapped at the edges of my body, warm in contrast to the cooler night air.

My mind drifted to Mace and what an absolute asshole he was. But even thinking that, I couldn't help but wonder what it would be like to kiss him, to feel him against me. I imagined him going down on me, his tusks rubbing against me as his tongue tenderly lapped at me, much like the water was doing. I slid my hands down my body.

Even as I seethed about how he'd acted towards me, I rubbed my pussy thinking about his incredible, strong hands. Wishing it was his fingers circling my clit. The waves of pleasure built up, my back arched and I tumbled over the cliff into a half-screaming orgasm. I wished Mace was there, coming with me, hate fucking ourselves into pleasurable oblivion.

I went back to my room feeling more relaxed than I had in ages. Once I was in bed, my mind circled back to Mace again, but now I was thinking about him and Aubrey. It didn't sound right, him being beaten down by a mean girl.

I tossed and turned for a few minutes before I finally got out my phone and searched for candid party pictures from the band's last tour. It didn't take long to spot the one who must be Aubrey.

Tall and slender with long, auburn hair, she hung on his arm like she'd grown there in almost every picture I found. She had sharp features and a smug look about her. She was pretty, but nothing really special. A standard attractive human.

What was it about her that had captivated him to such a degree? *Must be her personality*, I thought, though from what Frey had said, her personality wasn't much to talk about either.

I tucked my catty thoughts away and put down my phone. I stared at the ceiling for several heartbeats, wondering what kind of woman could ensnare the stoic orc so completely. Finally, I turned out the light and tried not to imagine myself hanging on Mace's arm like that.

I failed, though, and ended up imagining myself on a lot more than his arm. I sighed as I thrust my hands between my legs, and came again while thinking of how fucking hot Mace was even if he was a total asshole.

My alarm clock blared and I stumbled out of bed, rubbing visions of Mace out of my eyes. I threw on a robe and wandered into the main area of the suite. A breakfast feast was already laid out and my stomach growled. Drool filled my mouth at the sight of the plump strawberries and juicy looking melons.

As I piled fruit on my plate, Shawna came bouncing out of her room, all cheerful energy. She grinned at me and grabbed her own plate.

"I went ahead and ordered us a breakfast spread. It's part of the room deal."

I set my plate down and poured myself a cup of hot coffee, sniffing deep and appreciating the rich blend. "I'm absolutely ruined for regular hotel rooms now. Absolutely ruined. How am I supposed to live after experiencing this?"

Shawna laughed and sat down at the table. "So, I've been thinking, we're in a totally different position than we were with

Never Stop. We were authority figures with those kids, but with AxeBender? We're all colleagues."

"Yeah, I realized that we're working with grown-ass adults after we hung out with Frey last night. That was great. It was so much fun."

"And it was totally okay if the teeny-boppers got mad at us, because we were where the buck stopped. We weren't only running the show, we were literally the boss of them."

Even without my weird feelings for Mace, I really didn't want to treat the band like recalcitrant children. "I do not want to have a contentious relationship with the band, that would suck."

"Agreed! Maybe let's figure out some sort of 'bonding activities'?" Shawna did big air quotes, then furrowed her brow, thinking hard. "You know what would be fun? Games."

"Can you really see them playing games with us? A nice game of Uno?"

Shawna snorted at me. "You forget I've seen you play Uno. I've never seen someone quite as cutthroat and ruthless as you and a Draw Four card."

I rolled my eyes, but begrudgingly said, "I mean, you're not wrong."

"What I was thinking, was a friendly poker game."

"Oh, that could be fun. And all we need is chips and cards."

"Well, tonight's free," Shawna reminded me, "and this suite has a table plenty big enough for a poker game."

It was a perfect idea, and not just because I am very, very good at poker. "Okay, let's do this!"

"Awesome!" Shawna hopped up and grabbed the fancy hotel stationery. She pulled out some fancy pens from her purse and began making gorgeous calligraphy invitations for our "dinner and poker party."

"Wow, where did you learn to write like that? It's amazing."

Shawna shrugged and kept writing. "Yeah, I learned it as a kid. Was a thing my mom was big on."

Knowing how little Shawna liked to talk about her family situation, I dropped it.

While she finished up the invitations, I called the concierge and arranged for them to be delivered to the band members' rooms. I slipped the bellhop a fat tip when he arrived to pick them up. Yes, we could have texted, but that wouldn't have been *nearly* as much fun.

Then we got out our computers and did actual work, checking in on press events and reminding certain venue managers that we'd walk if they didn't follow our riders perfectly, even if the amount of Gatorade the band went through was truly unbelievable.

Following through on threats had never been necessary for me, but I was good at making it sound like I really meant it. And while Horace seemed weak in a lot of areas, he was strong in gossip and had killer notes about each venue. I felt a lot more kindly towards Horace after I realized how solid his notes were. Well, only a little more kindly. He was still scummy.

The first text we got accepting the invitation was from Frey:

Can't wait! This will be fun!

Then from Torch:

Sure, see you there. Everyone says I'm horrible at poker tho.

Jax and Clash responded with several texts each, all of the "we're going to take all your money" trash-talk variety. Then nothing. And nothing. And still utter silence from Mace. I tried not to let it bring my mood down.

Around four, Shawna and I knocked off work and began to set up for the party—which was also work, of course, as it was more for team-building than socializing. Shawna went to the store and got snacks and sodas and poker chips, while I ordered food from an Indian restaurant around the corner that the concierge said was phenomenal.

Then Shawna went back to the store after Frey sent a text:

Hey, any chance you guys have orc playing cards? I forgot to pick some up! It's not a big deal if you don't, it's just that they're a little bigger and sturdier. Of course I can handle it, but on the best of days, Jax will totally ham-hand them.

Of course we should have thought of that but it dropped right out of my mind. I shot a text back:

> *We'll grab some. We'll need them for the bus anyways. Plus when I clean out Jax, I don't want him to blame the cards.*

Orcs could play with human cards if they had too, but they'd have to concentrate the entire time on not dropping or tearing them. It's a whole lot easier for humans to play with orc cards than vice versa.

I tried not to think about Mace, or wonder why he hadn't texted to say if he was coming. I ordered extra food for him—since the band hadn't said what they wanted, we ordered a bunch of dishes from the "Orc Special" section of the menu. Lots of meat, lots of tuberous veggies, and way too spicy for most humans.

Finally, half an hour before everyone was due, we got a text from Mace that said:

OK.

Charming.

Chapter Twelve

MACE

I did not want to go to their poker party.

I was not going to go to their poker party.

And then half an hour before everyone else was supposed to be at the poker party I was absolutely not going to, Frey hammered on my door and informed me that I was, in fact, going to the poker party.

It's not that I'm scared of Frey. I'm not. She hasn't been able to beat me up since we were twelve, when I finally got bigger than her. So I'm not scared of her at all. It's just that I have very vivid *memories* of being scared of her.

Not that she was a bully, of course, she was just a whole lot tougher than me. She once broke a tree in half. Sure, I could do that too *now*. But she was eight. So while I'm not at all scared of her, at all, I still have a tendency to do what she says when she's mad. It's a habit, not actually fear.

So after our little chat, I picked up my phone and RSVP'd to the poker game right away.

Then I opened the hotel room's minibar and got out seven tiny bottles of alcohol. Human alcohol doesn't make orcs drunk, or anything like drunk. We have our own booze, and there was some of that in the minibar too, but I ignored it. I did not need to be drunk tonight, not when it took everything in me not to press Alexis against the wall and make her scream my name.

However, human alcohol does have one pretty major effect on orcs, one that I desperately needed right now. It kills our sex drive stone-cold dead. I opened the bottles and chugged them down. It would wear off, the same way it wears off in humans. But I was praying it would last long enough to get me through the party without making a fool of myself.

I was pretty sure I wouldn't hump Alexis's leg, but it had been a long time since I was with a woman, and sweet merciful, she was a lot of woman that I really wanted to be with.

By the time Frey knocked on my door again, I was pretty sure it had worked. The thought of Alexis didn't give me an instant hard-on, at least.

My head was a lot clearer as we rode up on the elevator. It was clear enough that it occurred to me to quietly ask Jax to somehow mention that I'd kicked some groupies out of my room and sent them to his and Clash's suite. He'd been covering my ass since we were kids.

He rolled his eyes at me. "Fine, I'll try and work it into conversation. *If* I can. I'm not gonna make it weird because you're weird about groupies, dude. Besides, we were full up and I ended up having to send them to Frey's orgy. Not that she actually takes advantage of anything these days."

Frey slapped him on the back of the head. "Fuck you."

We were all still laughing at Jax when we walked into Alexis' and Shawna's suite. Holy shit, it was a lot nicer than our rooms. Beyond a lot nicer. Enough nicer that I felt a little disgruntled.

"Whoa, nice digs, ladies!" Clash spun around, checking out the room.

"Yeah, Shawna worked her hotel mojo to get us a free upgrade to celebrate my promotion. No worries, it didn't come out of the budget." Alexis guided us into the heart of the suite.

I took in the massive space with a freaking fireplace. "Not that we begrudge you a nice room, of course, but damn, maybe rock stars should score rooms like this too, if we can afford them."

Shawna gave each of us a long, pointed up-down look. "Yeah, this ain't the kinda room we can afford to have trashed by a rollicking rock-star party. If you know what I mean."

We all changed the topic of conversation after that.

The food had been set out buffet-style, with the human food on a separate table. Indian is my favorite, if it's spicy enough, and this was—I could practically breathe fire. Alexis and Shawna seemed to enjoy playing hostess, pouring drinks and chattering.

"Okay, seriously now. Favorite snack combos? I know what you ask for in the riders and on the bus, but what's your go-to snack?" Alexis poured herself a coffee and glanced at Shawna. "Because I know Shawna's hangover favorite and it's so gross."

"Hey, just because you haven't experienced the healing power of coffee and Doritos doesn't mean it's gross!" Shawna attempted to defend herself, while the rest of us laughed. "We can't all love Cheetos and vanilla protein shakes, *Alexis*."

Jax made retching noises and Torch rolled his eyes.

Frey tossed a napkin at them. "I'm terribly boring, but anything peanut butter and chocolate with a salty side. Like peanut butter M&Ms and pretzels."

"My body is a temple so I don't put any of that crap in it." Torch flexed a bicep at the group and I found myself tensing up at the appreciative look in Alexis's eyes. *Mine!* If I hadn't pregamed with human booze, I definitely would have embarrassed myself.

Frey snorted and said, "Oh please! I know you sneak Funyuns when you think people aren't looking. It's not like we can't smell them from a million miles away. They're freaking onion-flavored rings. They reek."

If I hadn't prepared myself, I probably wouldn't have been able to take my eyes off the way Alexis's legs curved, and the way her breasts bounced. But as it was, I barely noticed those things and was able to notice how very funny she was, and smart too. She seemed to know a lot about every topic that came up.

Alexis didn't make a big deal about it, but I could feel the icy chill of her cold shoulder. Thank god for Jax, something I didn't often think.

"So there I was, the room was packed, wall-to-wall absolutely fucking *hotties*. I'm wiggling through, letting the ladies cop a feel, when I realize the woman in front of me has a weirdly lumpy chest, with fabric poking up from her shirt. Fabric I recognized." Jax threw his hands wide, emphasizing how far out the woman's chest was. "They were the custom boxers Clash got me for the holidays! I mean, I know it was a joke, but they're really comfy, and I liked them."

Frey snorted. "You mean the boxers festooned with your own goddamn face?"

"Yes! She muttered something about a souvenir, but handed them over. By the way, Mace, it was when I was kicking her out that the groupies you sent over popped up since you're *off women right now*. They were profoundly disappointed not to be able to claim they got to tear a piece off you. Real stunners, surprised you passed. I redirected them to Frey's crazy-ass orgy."

With that, I noticed that Alexis definitely thawed towards me. I don't know why it was so important to me that she realized I wasn't with anyone else, but it was. Rock god or not, her good opinion of me mattered.

The human alcohol I'd ingested meant I wasn't throbbing with the need to fuck her, but I still enjoyed her company. Every time I made her smile, it made me smile too.

She got more serious when it came time to play poker. She obviously took poker seriously, which was nice, since I did too. Jax and Clash like to talk big but for them, poker is about showing off. Frey and Torch enjoy it but don't care about winning, particularly, and it shows. When we're on tour I almost never get to play poker with anyone who plays really well.

It turned out she and Shawna were both pretty good, though Shawna played super tight and counted her chips more than anyone I've ever seen.

After about an hour and a half the others lost all their chips. I mean, it was very low stakes. They were only out fifty bucks. We were the only three left at the table. The other four sat on the couch near the fireplace, talking, and then as the game continued on and on they eventually said good night and left. A moment later I got a text from Frey.

> *I changed my mind, it's okay if you fuck the tour manager. You're made for each other, seriously."*

I laughed and shoved my phone into my pocket, grateful that orcs don't blush.

Chapter Thirteen

MACE

Alexis, Shawna, and I traded chips around the table for a while, but eventually Shawna started taking more and more of our chips until finally Alexis and I had the choice of folding or going all-in every hand. We struggled a bit and then everyone threw all their chips into the middle.

I had a ten-high straight I felt pretty good about, and it was better than Alexis' three of a kind, but Shawna blew us both out of the water with a full house.

Shawna seemed like she was struggling to be a good winner, but she didn't do a great job. She hooted and raked the chips in, then started stacking them and counting them, all but singing to them. She gently stroked the piles.

Alexis and I both stood and started gathering up chip bowls and glasses. "Is she always like this?" I asked Alexis, tilting my head towards Shawna.

"Oh, always," Alexis replied. "And she gets real sad when she loses a lot of chips, though she tries to hide it. She's fun to play with till the very end, though, and if she goes out early she's totally fine. And she's actually a much better winner than she appears."

I must have looked a little doubtful because she laughed. "No, really, check this out."

She turned towards the table and called, "Hey, Shawna, how do you want your winnings? Venmo? Cash?"

Shawna didn't even look up from the building she was making out of her chips. "Pick a charity. There's probably a children's shelter somewhere around here. Give it to them. Or I can look it up in a while."

Alexis turned back to me, eyebrows raised. "See? It's not about the actual money for her, like, at all."

I laughed. "I guess you're right. I definitely wasn't going to give the money to charity—"

"Me neither," Alexis agreed. "I was going to spend it all on either nail polish and face masks or booze, depending on my mood when I went to the store."

"I was going to spend it on nail polish, too," I said. "Orcs need a lot more nail polish than humans." I held up my hand to demonstrate. My nails were painted black, and it had taken a half a bottle of nail polish to make it happen. Black was a real pain in the ass, needing lots of layers to be opaque.

"Good point," Alexis said, putting her hand next to mine. "My nails have probably a quarter the surface area of yours.

Explains the nail polish allowance written into your contract. It doesn't explain why you guys go through so much Gatorade."

I wasn't about to tell her about the reasons orcs needed to hydrate. I would as soon die as to bring jizz into a perfectly nice conversation.

Standing so close to Alexis, her hand brushing mine and thinking about dehydrating activities, I realized the alcohol was definitely starting to wear off. She smelled good. Too good.

I pulled my hand away and if she noticed, she didn't show it. If anything she moved closer. "So what would you actually have spent it on?" she asked, serious now. I wished she wasn't so good at eye contact. It was making my heart hammer and my breath catch in my throat.

"Books," I said, honestly. "I'll sneak into a bookstore tomorrow or convince someone to grab me some more books. I've read all the books I brought with me on tour. Finished the last one earlier today."

She raised her eyebrows. Damn she was cute. "Do you know about e-readers?"

"Yeah, but—" I trailed off.

"But what?" Her eyes narrowed a little. "WHAT?"

I sighed and confessed. "Ebooks don't smell the same as real books."

She threw back her head at this and laughed, not mean, just surprised and maybe—happy?—at my answer.

Throwing back her head meant I could see her throat, and I knew I had to go before I did something I regretted. Like lick and nibble my way down her smooth, creamy skin.

"Well, um, it was fun," I said, walking quickly towards the door,

"Yeah, thanks for coming," Alexis said, sounding surprised and a little disappointed.

She followed me to hold the door open and I saw the hurt in her eyes at my abrupt departure. Feeling like a jerk, I forced a smile. "Thank you for having us over, it was really great."

I bent down to kiss her cheek, but somehow I missed, maybe she moved, anyway next thing I knew my lips were pressed against hers and it was like a cold drink of water when I'd been dying of thirst. The feel of her soft lips under mine, the smell of her, the electricity of our bodies so near each other. Desire zinged through my body and the effect of the human booze had definitely worn off.

I couldn't help myself, the slightest touch of her mouth made me wild with need and I fisted one hand in her hair and slid one hand down her back. Before it could turn into a real kiss, before I could get a taste of her, she pulled back with a bit of a gasp.

We stared at each other. I let her go and took a step back. Her eyes were wide and her hand drifted up to her plump lips. Fuck, I wanted to keep kissing her.

Instead, I said, "Well, bye," turned, and practically ran away. Didn't even wait for the elevator, just took the hotel stairs. I knew it was rude, but it was that or have my way with her right there on the floor. Which would have been a bad idea, for a lot of reasons, not least of which was the fact that Shawna was counting her chips a few yards away. And while she was pretty involved with her chips, even she would notice if I started acting like a wild, rutting animal.

Back in my room, I jerked off furiously, trying to get Alexis out of my system. It didn't work. I felt better for about a minute and then I was on my feet, pacing, trying to talk myself out of going back upstairs. I pounded a Gatorade. I needed to do something to get rid of this excess energy, this overwhelming desire—take a cold shower, maybe, or go work out.

Finally I realized I could do both at once. I threw on my swimsuit and went upstairs to the hotel pool.

Chapter Fourteen

MACE

The water wasn't as cold as I'd hoped, wanting to have my body short circuited from the endless waves of lust I'd been feeling since I met Alexis. Swimming still helped. A little. Okay, not much. Eventually I stopped and floated on my back at the deep end, trying to think of anything but *her*.

Failing that, I tried not to start stroking my cock again. I was still rock hard and fired up. Something about Alexis made me constantly ready to go. I thought about those full hips and what it would feel like to lift her up and spear her on my cock. I wanted to know what her face looked like when she was pushed to the edge over and over again, until I finally let her tumble over the cliff into a screaming orgasm. Was she a screamer?

I was jolted out of my lustful reverie by a small splash and a soft "Oh!" of surprise. I immediately went underwater, then found my feet and stood. It was a human pool—even in the deep end the water barely covered my chest. I looked up and expected to see some hotel guests who I'd have to avoid.

Soft light streamed in and highlighted a woman's face. Like my dreams come to life, Alexis stood in the shallow end. The water reached the tops of her thighs, and she wore a skimpy black swimsuit that managed to be both shockingly small and cover far more of her sweet curves than I liked. I couldn't tear my eyes off her. I drank her in, stunned into silence and enjoying how incredibly fucking hot she was.

Somehow, my cock got even harder and my mouth went dry.

"I—I'm sorry," she stuttered. I couldn't quite decipher her expression. Alarm? Fear? Something else? Her warm hazel eyes flashed gold at me and she licked her lips. If I didn't know any better, I'd think she was attracted to me, that she felt the same burning lust I felt. "I swim at night, sometimes," she continued, "and I didn't realize you were there, not until I was in the water, and—" her voice trailed off.

Without even realizing it, I'd been moving towards her, drawn to her. I forced my body to stop, the water at my waist, almost close enough to reach out and touch her. God, I wanted to touch her so bad. I wanted to know if the skin of her thighs was as soft and touchable as it looked. I wanted to grab her hand, tug her into the water and find out what it would sound like when she screamed my name while I was deep inside her. Thank god for the cover of the water so she couldn't see how aroused I was.

I smiled at her and tried to calm myself. I had to pretend like my cock wasn't jutting out from my body, desperately wanting to feel her heat wrapped around it. "No, I'm sorry," I said. All I had to do was get past her and get a towel around my waist. It probably still wouldn't hide a damn thing, but at least we could both pretend. "I was done swimming anyway, I can get out—" And then I stopped talking, because now she was moving towards me. I felt like a teenaged orc, ready to bust in my pants. I flexed my hands in the water and took a half step back. I didn't trust myself that close to her.

I couldn't look away from her gaze. It trapped me in place and oh, fuck me, she was so beautiful with her hair piled up on top of her head and the sideways light highlighting the side of her face.

But she kept moving towards me, her eyes wide. I could feel her warmth in the pool as she got close, finally stopping inches away, staring into my face, her lips slightly parted. I looked down at her, trying to resist, trying to fight the passion running through me, and then she licked her lips while glancing down at mine.

I groaned and pulled her toward me. Just one kiss, one single solitary kiss, so at least I knew what she tasted like. How she felt in my arms, before she inevitably slapped the dickens out of me for overstepping my bounds. No way would she let me do more than taste her once, she was far too amazing for a rock star with a terrible reputation. Even if she was everything I've ever dreamed of in a woman.

With one hand at her back, pressing her body against mine and one hand fisted in her hair, I dropped my lips to her mouth as her hands pressed against my chest. I thought she was going to push me away, I was ready for her to push me away. Instead, she parted her lips and her tongue flicked against my lips. She was kissing me, taking our kiss further and deeper.

Whatever control I had fled as our tongues tangled. I was utterly lost. This amazing, perfect woman was kissing me back!

Chapter Fifteen

ALEXIS

I don't know what came over me, but seeing Mace in the pool, the glint of water on his bare chest—I couldn't look away. The lights of the pool were dim, but enough to allow me to see his body was chiseled beyond what his too-tight tee-shirts suggested. Water dripped down his chest and I wanted to lap up the rivulets, to taste his beautiful emerald skin. To find out exactly how many rippling abs he had. It wasn't fair for him to be so ridiculously hot.

Without even realizing it, I moved closer to him in the water. By the time I got near, I couldn't help myself. I had to touch him, to kiss him. And once his lips met mine, I went up in flames and I forgot about everything but his touch. He clutched me to his body and I could feel the hard length of his cock against my belly. He was so hard and before I realized what I was doing, I let the water buoy my legs and I wrapped myself around him.

Our kiss kept going and as my legs wrapped around his waist, it opened me up to feeling his hard length against my aching center. I could tell he was thicker and longer than average. It would be so easy to flick aside my bathing suit, to let him fill me. My hands started moving down his chest when his hand dropped to my ass, pressing himself against me. I ground against his cock, each movement pushing me closer and closer to the edge.

The water moved against us as he strode forward, never relenting with his mouth, until my back hit the edge of the pool. He used the pool wall to push against me and stars sparked behind my eyes. I didn't care that someone might see us, or that I shouldn't be doing this. I moaned as he thrust against me.

He growled in my ear and nipped my neck. "This is everything I've ever wanted."

"Please, Mace." My face flushed. I sounded so needy, begging him for more. I edged closer and closer to an orgasm, I needed a little bit more from him. All I could think about was coming apart in his arms.

He growled into my ear, sending a lightning bolt of pure lust straight to my pussy. "Please what? Tell me what you want." I was so fucking close when he slowed his pace and pressed against me. "Tell me what you want."

Part of me knew we shouldn't be doing this, he'd thought I was a fucking groupie and had been hideously rude to me. Not to mention that I was pretty sure banging the talent was a huge no-no but I didn't care anymore. I needed him to push me over the edge.

The words came out of me in a rush, my cheeks reddened with embarrassment and want. "I want to come. Please, Mace, make me come." It was barely a whisper in his ear, but his low groan at my words showed that he heard me.

If I thought he had dragged me to the edge before, now he was relentless. His cock hot against me, pressing against my center, and hitting my clit with increasing frequency. My hands tightened against his shoulders and my nails dug in deep.

His hand dropped between our bodies and he rolled one of my nipples between his fingers. It was the last bit of stimulation I needed. My entire body went rigid as I tumbled over the cliff and felt waves of pleasure burst over me. My pussy clenched as I came harder than I've ever come before. It took everything I had not to scream as I writhed against his cock.

His hands were gentle on me as I rode out my orgasm. "Fuck, that was the hottest thing I've ever seen. Next time you come, I don't know if I want to be buried deep in your pussy or having you ride my face." My eyes fluttered open and I stared up into his eyes.

The cool water lapped against our blisteringly hot flesh and I was limp in his arms. But the words 'next time' bounced around in my head until I shivered. As I came back to myself, my stomach dropped. What had I done? I never should have lost control like this, with him of all people.

But then Mace nuzzled my neck and whispered in my ear. "Please don't get in your head about it. I see you pulling back, it's in your face."

I shivered again in his arms, finally lifting my eyes up to his. They blazed at me, desire swirling in them. I bit my lower lip, trying to figure out what the hell was I supposed to do.

"How about we just see where this goes, okay?" His voice was deep and made me throb between my legs. I knew what I should do was unwind myself from around his body. Put on a pleasant smile and blow him off like I did with all the dudes I'd ever worked with. But the rigid length of him still pressed against my core and I was weak against the entreaty in his eyes.

I nodded. "Okay. I shouldn't be doing this but—" My voice trailed off. Could I admit to him how much I wanted him? How I wanted him so badly that I was ready to throw caution and everything I'd ever thought about workplace romance into the wind? I'm sure whatever we were doing would burn out fast enough. He was a rock star with literal groupies doing everything in their power to get him between their legs. He'd get bored of me quickly and I'd at least have a story to keep me warm at night.

It had been way too long since I'd had anything close to a romance. The closest I'd been was the year before when I thought I had a pretty good on-line romance going with a handsome guy named Lance, only to find out I'd been catfished by an old lady with seven pet parrots.

But for once, someone wanted me. Not trying to get close to my sister. Or trying to get backstage. Or trying to use my industry connections. Or trying to amuse her pet parrots.

For a moment, I wondered if it was simply that I was convenient. That I was *here* and available. But the gentle touch of his hand on my cheek and the way he asked about us going forward made his intentions clear. He wanted me. He wanted me *again*. Getting laid was never going to be a problem for Mace, even if he wasn't a rock star. But he could have had beautiful women who weren't nearly as much of a pain in his ass as I was.

And fuck me, I wanted him so much. I wanted to ride his face, his cock, his hands, his everything.

Chapter Sixteen

*A*LEXIS

We broke apart awkwardly and I looked up at him. "So uhm, did you—you know?"

He grinned at me, a mischievous glint in his eyes. "Did I? What, exactly?"

My cheeks burned red as I stumbled over the words, "Did you, you know, uhm, come? I was kind of distracted." I couldn't keep my eyes on his, and stared a hole in his shoulder.

But he chuckled as I considered dying of embarrassment. His voice was low and rumbled with amusement. "I was completely focused on you, on your pleasure. It's easy for guys, I can take myself in hand as needed."

Yup, I was definitely going to sink to the bottom of the pool and never emerge again. I forced the words out. "Would you like a, uhm, hand?"

He threw his head back and laughed. "Sweetness, more than anything I want your hands on me." I finally looked back up into his eyes and about burst into flames at the heat in them. But before I could make a move towards him, to touch him, a group of giggling girls burst through the pool doors and I pushed away from Mace instead of back into his arms.

Thank god they hadn't arrived a minute earlier.

He sighed and smiled at me. "We should definitely get out of here before they realize who I am."

But it was too late. A shriek erupted from one of the girls and they all started pointing and giggling some more. They were definitely wildly underage and I was wondering if I was going to have to start calling parents. But he was so sweet with them. They had stars in their eyes and Mace took lots of selfies with them. He was absolutely charming and sweet, and despite the fact that we'd been in a passionate embrace, he was incredibly patient with them.

I was absolutely a goner for him. I'd completely misjudged him as a sleazebag.

He was kind as he managed to peel away from them, saying, "And now I need to walk my manager to her room. It was lovely meeting you. Have a safe swim."

And then we were in the elevator, watching the numbers count down to our floor. I had no idea what to say. Should I invite myself into his room? Would Shawna freak out if I didn't show up until morning? I wish I knew how to manage something like this. I was completely out of my element.

But he wasn't. He walked me to my room and we stared at each other hungrily. At first I thought he might be as unsure as I was about what to do next, but the look in his eyes made me think he was deciding whether to fuck me right there in the hall.

My heart sped up as I fumbled with the door. I wanted him to take me right there and then, I wanted to drag him to my bedroom by the tusks and spend all night learning his body by heart. But the idea of facing Shawna in the morning, the idea of the band finding out—it was more than I could handle.

"Good night," I whispered.

To my relief, he smiled, looking disappointed but not angry or upset. "I'll see you tomorrow," he said and there was a passionate promise behind the words. "Sweet dreams. Make sure you lock the door behind you. Better safe than sorry."

I hated closing the door on him, but I did and threw the dead bolt. I floated into my room, stripped out of my swimsuit, and ran through the shower. I was on cloud nine when I crawled into bed. I wished I'd crawled into bed next to Mace, but I drifted off with a smile on my face.

The next morning, I finally came to as Shawna pounded on my door.

"Wake up, princess!"

I groaned and sat up, rubbing my eyes. "Fuck you, Shawna, let a girl sleep!" I'd been having an amazing dream involving Mace and his tongue.

"Uhm, the bus leaves in, like, fifteen minutes. I'm assuming you'd like to be on it."

"Oh shit!" I grabbed my phone and looked at the time. I'd slept in crazy late. "Okay, it doesn't leave in fifteen minutes, that was cruel to say."

"Considering how precise you like to be in your packing? It might as well be five minutes."

I grimaced at her. "Well, fine, you're not wrong." It was hard living out of a suitcase and I definitely preferred keeping my bags in a specific order, that way I always knew where everything was. I threw myself out of bed, grateful I'd taken a shower the night before.

Satisfied that I was getting up, Shawna wandered off, while I threw myself into clothes, pausing only to switch out from cozy cotton panties to a lacy scrap of fabric. Not for any specific reason, just, you know, *in case.* So I'd feel confident and not at all because of the dream I had about Mace ripping them off with his tusks.

I tried to shove my life back into my suitcases, neatly.

But time was ticking by, and I knew I had to suck it up and plan on repacking at the next stop. I flew around, shoving things into my bags and Shawna popped back up with a coffee and danish.

She thrust them into my hands and said, "Eat. Drink."

"I don't have time!" I was a little panicked that I was going to make the bus late. It was the last thing I wanted to do, after we'd been getting along with the band so well. Thinking of Mace, maybe I'd been getting along a little too well.

Shawna rolled her eyes at me. "Take two minutes. You'll feel much better once you've had some coffee."

Something in her voice made me sit down and drink the coffee. Annoyingly, she was right. With my coffee and food inside me, a burst of energy zinged through me. We flitted around the spacious rooms and I was tempted to tell Shawna all about what happened with Mace the night before.

But I couldn't, I didn't want her to look at me differently. Holy shit, we'd barely started on the tour and I was hooking up with the lead singer. I could hardly believe how incredibly unprofessional I was being. Tour managers do not fool around with members of the band. It just isn't done. I'd acted like a besotted groupie.

Still, as much as I tried to berate myself, I couldn't stop thinking about how it felt when Mace was pressed up against me. My whole body was tingling and zinging with electricity, and every few minutes I'd remember a detail of the night before and I'd shiver with delight.

I decided not to tell Shawna. Yet. But I swore to myself that I wouldn't let this drag on for long without confiding in her. Friend code wouldn't allow it.

Besides, she was going to figure out something was up, because I definitely wasn't acting normal. I was too damn happy.

Shawna put on some AxeBender while we packed, and I thrilled at the sound of Mace's voice. I sang along, and when I did, my clothes zoomed into my suitcase without my even having to point. The magic was shooting out of me, in a way that was both totally foreign and also distantly familiar.

It had been like this for a while, when I was a teenager, before my sister started winning awards and scholarships and everything became about how I wasn't as good as her at magic. It was true, I wasn't. Few witches are—not even my parents, at this point. But I'd been pretty good.

Somehow the comparisons squashed the magic out of me. I didn't know why I was more powerful this morning—it's not like it was the first time I'd ever gotten sexy with a guy, after all—but I enjoyed the power buzzing through my veins.

I was really sad to walk away from the incredibly luxurious suite. We weren't likely to repeat that particular experience and I did not hate being pampered like that.

But I was looking forward to getting on the bus. To being on the bus with Mace. I'm sure the opportunity to fool around wouldn't arise, but if it did? Another shiver ran through me as I thought about wrapping my hand around his cock, pumping it, feeling it throb and hearing him moan. I could totally give him a handy under a blanket. No one would notice. *Hopefully*.

Chapter Seventeen

ALEXIS

My mood dampened when Shawna and I got on the bus and waited for the band members. What if he'd told all of them? What if they were all laughing about me right now? Well, not Frey. I was certain she wouldn't do that. But the others might. At the very least, the respect I'd won from them would wither away. What if the record execs found out? I started to panic a little at the thought.

Hopefully the cold light of morning would make both of us more sensible. I needed to talk to him about it, so we both knew where we stood. That clearly it was a one-off and we'd lost our heads. He'd go back to dripping in groupies and I'd crawl into my solitary, cold bed and not think at all about how his abs had abs. And that V of his adonis belt totally didn't beg me to lick it.

I almost couldn't look at the band as they climbed aboard, but I had to know if they knew. As soon as I saw their faces, air whooshed out of my lungs in relief. They were friendly, cheerful, and *completely* oblivious. No side eyes, no smirks, no knowing glances.

Mace brought up the rear, and his face was perfectly normal too, as he climbed the steps and ducked his head a little. He smiled shyly and said good morning. You'd never have guessed I'd been wrapped around him the night before. But then our eyes met and a jolt of hot desire shot through me. I half swooned, he winked and looked away. Warm sunshine ran in my veins, I was bursting with happiness. I could have floated right out of my seat. I gripped the arm rests and made sure my butt was firmly planted in the chair.

I tried hard to get my brain under control. It was a one-off. We weren't a thing, an item, a couple. It was a solitary tryst and it wasn't going to happen again. We could go back to being friends, I told myself over and over. But it was no use.

Once we hit the road, I tried to think of an excuse, *any* excuse, to wander back and chat with him. I couldn't think of anything that wouldn't be utterly transparent, wouldn't make it obvious I was just trying to be close to Mace. Mace and his thick, strong arms. Wrapping around me, lifting me onto his cock.

As I dithered and fantasized, his voice boomed from behind me: "Hey, Shawna, Alexis, either of you like crosswords? None of these guys do and I could use some help!"

Shawna rolled her eyes. "Finally. Someone who will do crosswords with you so you'll stop bugging me. As if I'm going to know a seven-letter word for 'nerd' or whatever."

I pretended to give her a dirty look and rose, trying to keep my face normal. I staggered unsteadily down the rows of seats, bouncing from one side to another, before I finally made it to where he was sitting, almost in the very back of the bus.

"I love crosswords," I said truthfully, sinking down into the seat next to him. He really did have a book of crosswords open in front of him, and a ballpoint pen in his hand. I hadn't been sure if it wasn't an excuse to get me to sit with him. Although we hadn't hung out enough for him to know that I liked crossword puzzles. Not to brag, but I was really good at them, I'd been doing the *New York Times* puzzle every day for years.

"Great. I need a nine-letter word for 'organ cover.' Second letter 'P,' last letter 'S.'"

I pondered for a moment, rolling different words and concepts in my mind, until one popped up. "Epidermis."

"Yes, thank you!" he cried, writing it in. Damn, how was it ridiculously sexy that he did crossword puzzles in ink? It was unfair that even his hands were big and sexy, flexing around the pen, making it look puny in his hands.

I couldn't figure out how to bring up last night, so we sat like that for another hour or so, finishing one crossword and starting another. Every few clues we'd be reminded of some story. We were talking as much as solving puzzles. Fuck, despite our bad start, I really liked this guy. He was funny. And most of his stories involved poking fun at himself. He wasn't the arrogant rock star I'd pictured in my head.

Eventually the crosswords were forgotten and we talked, talked about everything under the sun. We seemed to fall into a perfect conversational pattern together almost at once, no one interrupting or talking over the other, taking turns telling stories, never falling into lecture mode or dominating the conversation. And best of all, our senses of humor matched perfectly.

We liked a lot (but not all) of the same movies, and many (but not all) of the same books. I was shocked at how much we had in common, considering how different our lives were. We'd both grown up on the west coast, with immigrant grandparents. We both had big extended families, though I only saw mine on major holidays.

I have a sister who I loathe; he was an only child but grew up on the same block with all his bandmates, making him feel like he not only had a sister and three brothers, but three extra sets of parents as well.

"Which means," he said, "I have six more people looking after me, but also six more people to disappoint. More than six, in fact. I failed chemistry in the tenth grade, and the next day, *Torch's grandmother* called me on the phone to deliver a lecture on responsibility. No lie."

I burst out laughing at the thought. "What did you say?"

"I said 'yes ma'am' and 'no ma'am' and promised to do better, of course. Torch's grandmother is *terrifying*."

"She sounds like my kinda lady. "

"Yeah, you looked just like her when you lectured us about trashing hotel rooms. I couldn't believe the resemblance."

I stifled a laugh and narrowed my eyes at him. "Oh good. I was going for 'scary grandmother'."

Chapter Eighteen

ALEXIS

He grinned at me and said, "So, what was your family like? Are you close with them?"

I tried not to grimace and stuffed down my standard, impulsive joke answers, about how my sister was born with a magic wand in her hand, and I was born with a letter of apology in mine. As hard as it was, Mace made me want to open up and share about myself. I took a deep breath and shrugged.

"Well, to be honest, it was really hard growing up as a witch with an older sister who was so much better at magic than I was. According to my parents, better at literally everything than me." I looked away from him and stared out the window, unable to stop myself now that I'd gotten going. "She was a star pupil all through school and everyone expected that I'd follow in her footsteps. It got really bad when she started winning big awards and things. Because it wasn't going to happen like that for me.

I was okay at magic, I wasn't bad at it or anything, but I wasn't great. I wasn't special like her, I didn't blow away my teachers."

Mace took my hand in his, letting me get it all out. I swallowed hard and pressed on. "But because she was amazing, I had to go to the same extra advanced classes every Tuesday and Thursday after school. Except I was *average*. It was mostly me getting tutored and not being allowed to follow any of my own interests. Truthfully, I'd desperately wanted to just play field hockey and hang out with my friends. But the rage on my mom's face at even the hint that I'd drop those stupid classes shut that idea right down."

Mace squeezed my hand and the warmth in his grip helped anchor me back in reality. "My parents said I didn't apply myself. My sister would *defend* me saying it wasn't my fault I was a talentless hack and not very smart."

His hand spasmed around mine and his voice was low and growly, tinged with anger. "Um, that doesn't sound like she was actually defending you."

"Yeah, it never felt like that to me either. But in a weird way it made it hard to defend myself, liked I'd be agreeing with her that I was just a dumb loser. Eventually, I stopped trying. I went to magic class, but I didn't try to do well, particularly. And then, when I got old enough, I found a career as far removed from that world as possible. Doing something that I actually enjoyed, for once."

"So what does your sister do now? Please tell me she still lives in your parents' basement. Or that she's trapped in some boring corporate witch job."

I bit my lip and hated to tell him how successful my terrible sibling was. "No, actually—" It honestly killed me a little to say it, but I also figured it would be better for him to know now. It always came out, eventually. "She's Lucinda Travers."

His eyes widened. "Seriously?"

Fuck, I knew it, I knew he'd be impressed with her and think I was a total bitch for hating her.

"Yup," I muttered, waiting for him to ask, "THE Lucinda Travers??" followed by a list of her endless accomplishments, starting with her many degrees, moving on to the time she rescued an entire of bus full of nuns and orphans, listing the countless wars she's ended and natural disasters she's averted, and finishing with her constant TV appearances, in which she cures disease and finds lost relatives and buried treasure.

But he didn't do any of that. "God damn, she's the *worst*. We used to have a drinking game where we'd watch her show and take a drink every time she complimented herself, but had to stop after Jax got so drunk he forgot how to play guitar. Living in the same house as her must have been awful."

And then he stopped talking because I'd launched myself onto him. I pressed my lips against his and every thought of telling him our hookup was a one-time deal disappeared. I lost myself in the moment, plundering his mouth and kissing him like I'd never kissed anyone before. I couldn't believe I'd finally met someone who didn't at least start out thinking my sister was the greatest person on the planet.

I finally broke away, breathless. "Thank you." My cheeks were flushed and I awkwardly came back to myself. I'd jumped on the poor guy and if anyone on the bus had looked back, we would have been completely busted.

He laughed. "No, thank *you*. I'll insult her a lot more if this is the reaction. Her nose is dumb, for instance. And when she walks, her elbows move weird."

A giggle bubbled up from deep within me. Mace was nothing like what I expected. *Everyone* loved my stupid sister. "Save it. And by save it, I don't mean don't insult her. I want it to last. Tell me one every hour or so." Then I felt sheepish. "That probably sounds epically petty. But you wouldn't believe how often people gush over her and tell me how incredibly great she is. All I can think about is how she's insanely mean to me. And our parents have never once responded to anything I've done well without pointing out that Lucy does it better. Thanksgiving is a waking nightmare."

Mace tapped my nose. "You know what? Fuck your sister and double fuck your parents. You should come home with us for Thanksgiving," he gestured at the band in front of us, "instead of putting all your mental energy into not murdering your family with the carving knife. It's really fun! We shut down the block, move a bunch of tables into the street and all our families eat together. There's always room at our table. And I bet Torch's grandma will adore you."

He said it super casually, and my heart sped up, imagining a future where it made sense to go to his family holiday celebrations. I smiled, treating it like something Mace was saying offhand. He was trying to be nice to me, which was really sweet. But there is no way a guy I'd fooled around with once—well twice if you count the kiss we just had—would invite me to join his family at a holiday months away.

"Now," he said, his bright blue eyes sparkling and a cheerful grin on his face. "I think we should find out exactly how grateful you are to me for seeing past your sister's facade and all."

He put his hand on my knee, running it slowly up my thigh. A shiver rolled up my spine and my pussy clenched with desire. I wanted nothing more than to throw my leg over his and mount him right then and there. But then Shawna erupted into loud laughter and that dumped a massive bucket of ice-cold water on my lust for Mace.

I took a shuddering breath and pulled myself together. I put my hand on his, stopping him midway up my thigh. Fuck, I was so wet for him I could barely think, but there was no way everyone else on the bus wouldn't notice if we went beyond a kiss. We were lucky no one had seen the enthusiastic kissing.

"Not here." My voice shook with need. "It's not you, I swear, but I really don't want people to know about whatever this is yet. A tour manager getting together with a band member isn't great when they've known each other for ages. A tour manager fooling around with a lead singer four days after joining the tour? Seriously frowned upon." It's not exactly what I'd meant to say. I'd meant to say that of course we were going to stop whatever this was. Except I could still feel the heat of him on my lips and I wanted to taste him again. One more time.

"So we have to keep it a secret?" he asked, a smile twitching his lips. "Be super subtle and crafty? So, say, if I can't stand it anymore and I have to touch those tits, I need to do it like this?" He casually reached up and grazed the back of his hand across my nipples. I tried not to whimper, desire flooding through my body again. I squeezed my legs together, trying to keep from pouncing on him.

"And if I notice your neck needs to be kissed, I should pretend I'm telling you a secret instead?" He put his face close to my ear, licking the top of my neck and gently biting my earlobe. "Like this?" he whispered.

It took everything I had to push him away, and this time he stayed away, still smiling but not touching me. "Okay," he said. "I'll wait. I'll wait till we're alone before ripping off your panties, burying my head between your legs, and licking your pussy until you scream."

Yeah, I could get on board with that suggestion. He wasn't even touching me and I burned for him. I peeked down the aisle at everyone else on the bus. They were all goofing off and not paying one bit of attention to us. An idea sparked in my thoughts, a way I could have my cake and, well, have it eat me too.

Chapter Nineteen

*A**LEXIS*

My mind flew back to high school, when I still learned new magicks. If I wanted to read a book at the back of the classroom, there was one spell that always worked to keep my teacher from noticing me.

Back then, I felt capable of doing more than the simplest spells. It was probably one of the hardest spells I'd learned and I hadn't attempted it in a long time. As an adult, it wasn't something I would normally have bothered with. I was worried it wouldn't work but something about being near Mace made me feel powerful and competent.

"Let me try something," I said. I turned and faced the front of the bus. I waved my hand, tracing a rune in the air. I concentrated, muttering the incantation under my breath. The space in front of our seats turned shimmery, like we were looking out from inside a soap bubble.

"What did you do?" he asked.

My blood fizzed with joy, realizing I'd successfully cast a spell I'd long since put behind me. "I made a mirage. If anyone looks back here, it will look like we're sitting a foot apart, doing crossword puzzles. No one will see us, or hear us. So, now," I smiled wickedly and reached up to hook a finger into each of his tusks, gently pulling his head downwards, "what were you saying about making me scream?"

His face almost split in two with a grin and his eyes lit up, a gray ring around the blue pinning me to my seat. He reached down and flipped the armrest between us up. "Let's get a little more comfortable." He flexed his massive arms and I was suddenly in his lap.

One massive hand fisted in my hair as his mouth descended on mine. If last night we'd been tentative and growing bolder, this kiss was all fire and heat. And I went up in flames as he explored my mouth with his tongue. His tusks should have made kissing difficult, but it was another way for him to tease me. The sensation of them rubbing against my lips was erotic as hell. As his intensity increased I couldn't stop the moan that erupted from deep in my throat.

He pulled back slightly and whispered, "Can they hear us?" All I could do was nod helplessly against him. Fuck, I had to be quiet. Really, really quiet. He nibbled his way to my neck, and delicately licked the shell of my ear. Instant panty melter, feeling his smooth tusks against my neck. His other hand slid down my arm, then across my chest. A gentle touch I could barely feel that drove me absolutely wild. I tried to press against him, but he pulled back, only letting me have the softest of touches.

Our mouths fought each other and before I knew it, in my distraction, he'd taken my hands and pulled them behind me, holding them easily with one of his massive hands. Not being able to move my arms made me burn hotter. I thought I was going to melt right through the bus seat. He finally let go of my hair and traced his fingers down my cheek, down my neck and finally, with an agonizing, tormenting slowness, he circled my nipple, teasing it until it was a rock-hard nub.

I groaned against his mouth, while he tormented my body, his thumb tickling my nipple while his tongue swirled in my mouth as he cradled me. His hand dropped to my bare knee and I was beyond grateful I'd decided to wear a skirt. His hand first slid up the outside of my leg, dragging the fabric up with it. Each movement was delicious agony to my sensitized skin. He cupped my ass and squeezed. I couldn't help but wiggle against him.

He broke the kiss and again, in a low tone meant only for my ears, asked, "Can you manage to keep quiet?" I nodded as we stared into each other's eyes. His hand slipped back down to my knee, then pushed my legs open. I felt dirty and wanton. Spread wide, having to stay silent so the rest of the band didn't hear us. I shivered in anticipation as his hand moved up my inner thigh, gently kneading his way until his fingers danced over my damp panties.

Now it was his turn to groan. "Fuck, look at how wet for me you are already." He stroked me through my panties as I arched against his hand.

He teased me until I couldn't take it anymore and shamelessly started begging him for more. "Please, Mace, please."

"Please what?"

"Touch me."

"I am touching you. Tell me exactly what you want."

All shame and doubt were long gone. "Please, Mace, touch my pussy. Make me come."

A low growl came from him as I spoke and his hand slipped under the edge of my panties. His thick fingers parted the seam of my sex and stroked up to my clit. He lazily circled my clit until my breath came out in pants and I was bucking against his hand. A finger slipped into my core, stretching me as he added another finger.

"Fuck, baby, you're so tight. I can't wait until you're strangling my dick with your pussy."

His fingers dipped in and out of my center and his grip tightened on my wrists. He shifted his hand so his thumb could continue circling my clit and my thighs started shaking. My passion built and I whispered, "Fuck, I'm going to come."

I struggled to keep my sounds under control and he crushed my mouth beneath his, muffling my shout as I exploded around his fingers, my whole body shaking with my release. He brought his hand up to his mouth and slowly licked each finger, never breaking eye contact.

"Fuck, you're delicious. I need to taste your sweet pussy." He eased me back against the window, pausing to make sure I was comfortable before kissing his way down my neck. He dropped to his knees, pushed one leg wide and lifted the other to his shoulder. He let go of my wrists and I twined my hands through his hair as he pressed his lips between my legs.

The first swipe of his flattened tongue as he started at the bottom and licked through my panties to my clit sent my hips bucking. I was still so sensitive from my last orgasm, I wasn't sure if I could handle him. But his growl into me sent my heartbeat racing and I ground myself against his face. He pressed me back into the seat as his fingers flexed on the delicate fabric of my panties.

As his fingers shredded the lace, it was all I could do not to scream his name. He tucked the scraps into his back pocket and grinned up at me.

He leaned forward and growled in my ear. "Skip wearing panties. I'm going to destroy them all. I want to know your pussy is available for my tongue any time."

Then he dropped his face into the apex of my thighs and thrust his tongue into my core and my whole body went tight as he fucked me with his mouth. All I could do was hang on and ride his face.

He licked upwards and flicked at my clit until my thighs started shaking again. The only thing I could focus on was the heat of his mouth and keeping quiet. A single slip and someone would walk right through my mirage and see me splayed out, screaming for more.

He sucked my clit into his mouth and I had to let go of his head to press my hands against my mouth. I could feel the building waves of desire racing through my body and I was helpless against his assault. He pressed two deliciously thick fingers into my core.

I bucked against his hand and mouth and somehow managed not to scream as waves of pleasure shot through me and I came so hard I almost blacked out. I was vaguely conscious of him pulling my skirt down and pulling me into his lap as I rode out my orgasm.

I wasn't sure how much time had passed before I finally pried my eyes open and looked up at him. A crooked smile was on his face and I realized I could still feel how hard he was under my hip. I wiggled slightly, enjoying the lust that flashed in his eyes. I twined my arms around his neck and pulled him in for a kiss, enjoying the taste of me on his tongue and lips.

His hardon throbbed against me and I ground against him until his hands tightened on me and his breath came out in a pant. I shifted my body, until I was straddling him, centering myself over his thick cock and rocking my hips until his hands grabbed my ass. He pressed me down, stilling my motion.

His voice was a low growl and despite having come twice, I felt my core throb with neediness.

"Baby, I need you to stop unless you want me to plunge into you, make you scream and shatter that mirage that is barely keeping everyone out of our business."

Chapter Twenty

MACE

She grinned down at me with a wicked glint in her eye and pressed a kiss on my lips. I could still taste her sweet honey and despite thinking I was as hard as possible, my dick somehow stiffened even further. If she pushed me much further, I was going to fuck her until she screamed, ruining all her little secret keeping. I didn't give a fuck if anyone saw me make her mine. I wanted everyone to know, to know that I'd claimed her and she was *mine*.

Before I could flip her to her knees and fill her greedy cunt, she started kissing her way down my neck, pausing only to nibble where my collarbone met my throat. She was sliding down my body and all I could think about was her amazing curves and the look on her face when she came. I didn't realize her intentions until she sank to her knees and popped the button on my jeans.

I grabbed her hands. "You don't have to do this. I wanted to pleasure you."

She looked up at me, her lips pouty and full. "I want to do this, I've been wanting to know what you taste like since last night."

Before I could think to argue or drag her back up, she reached under the waist of my jeans and drew my cock out. I usually went commando and was thanking my lucky stars that I'd continued that trend today. She pulled the zipper until I was completely free, nothing between me and her luscious mouth. She licked her lips and precum pooled at the tip of my cock.

I was torn, I didn't want her to feel like she had to do anything other than accept pleasure, but sweet merciful Luna, I wanted her lips wrapped around me more than I'd ever wanted anything else in my life. She grasped the root of my dick and took a long, lingering lick across the top of my cock, flicking her tongue down the slit. *Holy shit, I'm not going to last but a minute in her mouth.*

When she twirled her tongue around the crown and slowly drew me into her lips, it took everything in me not to grab her and fuck her face. But it was even better to see my cock slowly disappear between her lips, her mouth stretched by my girth. Then her cheeks hollowed as she drew back, sucking me hard. Stars glittered around the edge of my vision as I fought the desire to shoot my load down the back of her throat.

Never surprise a woman with that. An orc should especially not surprise a human woman with that much come. Although it would be fucking hot to see her take everything I had to give.

She sank back down my cock, taking me even deeper into her mouth. I couldn't stop my hips from jerking a little as the sensation drove me to the edge. She wrapped both hands around me, stroking upward as she pulled back. Each time I thought she'd release me, she would pull me deeper and deeper into her mouth, until she had more of my cock that any woman had ever taken before.

I kept my hands gripping the armrests and they cracked a little as I tried to channel my urges away from spurting down Alexis's throat. She was going to be the death of me.

As she drew me deeper still, I hit the back of her throat and groaned at the picture of perfection. Those lush, fuckable lips stretched around my thick green cock. Her tongue, pressing against the bottom of my dick and the intense heat of her mouth. I wasn't going to be able to stop myself.

I tried to reach for her shoulders. "I can't," I whispered. "You have to stop. I'm gonna come."

I swear to god she grinned up at me and went faster, her hands moving with her mouth and I was utterly lost. It took everything in my power not to roar as my cock exploded down Alexis's throat. Despite jacking off multiple times this morning, I felt like I was coming forever, absolutely filling her with my seed. And she took it, spurt after spurt, she took it, her eyes never leaving mine. Finally, I collapsed back, utterly spent.

I looked down on a vision of perfection. Alexis released my cock and a slight drizzle of pearly white cream seeped out of her mouth. The red of her lipstick was smeared as her tongue darted out, capturing the little bit of come she hadn't taken. Like she wasn't going to let any of my essence escape. My heart clenched, I'd never felt anything like this before.

It wasn't just screwing around. I didn't only want to fill her sweet little pussy and watch our juices drip out of her. I wanted to do crossword puzzles and play poker with her. I wanted to snuggle up to her while watching a movie. Okay, and I also wanted to bend her over literally everything and fuck her until we both were completely satisfied.

I was head over heels in a way that no other woman, not even freaking Aubrey, had ever made me feel. Alexis was mine and I was going to mark her in every way I could until the tour was over, then I was going to carry her off. Before I could follow my thoughts further, she rose up, smiling at me.

"I'm going to slip into the bathroom, clean up a little." She glanced behind her. "Oh thank god, the mirage held. I kind of totally forgot about it. I was, uhm, distracted?"

I grinned at her like a loon.

She slipped off and my smile faded. I knew she wanted to stay on the downlow, but how was I going to keep my feelings from showing? Just keeping my hands to myself was going to be a struggle. Her soft skin begged to be stroked. She deserved to be on my arm and acknowledged as mine, not a dirty little secret. Although sneaking around was also hot as fuck.

By the time the bus reached the arena for that night's show, we'd straightened our clothing and cleaned up in the bathroom and I was reasonably certain no one was going to guess what we'd been up to.

Chapter Twenty-One

*A**LEXIS*

Once Shawna and I were alone in the green room, she asked what Mace and I had talked about. I shrugged. "Not much." I wasn't really lying—at a certain point, we weren't doing a lot of talking. "We mostly did crosswords. He's pretty good at them."

Shawna said, "Uh huh. Just crosswords?" She took a slight sniff and raised an eyebrow. She couldn't possibly know what we'd been up to. Humans don't have that kind of sense of smell.

It felt wrong, not spilling everything to her like I usually did, but it also didn't feel right, asking Mace to keep whatever we were doing to himself and then not doing the same. Besides, I was still a little embarrassed to admit I was banging a band member. I wasn't sure how to reconcile my feelings for Mace and my worry about my job. Everything was a lot easier when I was managing a group of tweens.

This was the first band of adults I'd been in charge of, and I was already sleeping with one of them. Well, not sleeping with Mace, not yet, but I wanted to be and instead of putting a stop to our madness, I deep-throated him in the back of a bus.

Damn, maybe my family was right and I wasn't cut out for being in charge of anything.

Shawna and I went around to the side stage to watch the show again. I'd never done that much before, but I'd never enjoyed music like I enjoyed AxeBender's. I couldn't resist dancing a little, but when Shawna tried to pull me down to the concert floor, I resisted like always. I was here as a professional, not a fan, and while the band might possibly still respect me if I acted like one, the vendors and venue managers likely would not.

We went back to the hotel after the show and I was relieved to see that this time Shawna hadn't scored us a suite. It would be a lot easier to sneak around and spend time with Mace if we didn't have to tiptoe through a shared space.

Another band was staying at the same hotel, as sometimes happens on tours, and there was an absolute rager of a party going by the time we arrived. Shawna and the rest of the band decided to join in the fun. I did a big fake yawn, said I was tired and that I'd see them in the morning. I went to my room and started pacing.

What if Mace didn't show up? What if he did? I was getting so anxious I could barely breathe. I had no idea what to do, should I text him? Was that too forward? I twisted my hands together and kept pacing and staring at the bed. I wanted Mace so bad but had no idea how to navigate whatever the fuck it was that we were doing.

But I didn't have to wait long before there was a tap on my door. My pulse skyrocketed and my mouth went dry. I shook my hands out and tried to look cool. I checked the peephole with my heart in my throat, half wanting it to be someone else. But I could see Mace standing in the hallway.

I pulled the door open and found Mace now leaning on the door frame, looking forlorn. "I hurt my hand," he said, holding it up. It looked fine. "I hurt my hand by touching something hot and it hurt so much I had to leave the party. And since you're the tour manager, I figured maybe you could fix it."

I smiled, grabbed him by the shirt, and yanked him into the room. "I'll see what I can do."

He kicked the door shut behind him and threw the hotel latch. There was a gleam in his eye as we moved to the middle of the room, near the foot of the bed. My hands shook with the intensity of his gaze. I was already wet and ready for him. He was so much bigger than I was, taller and broader than even your average orc. I thought back to getting busy on the bus and wondered for a hot minute if getting his cock in me was even going to be possible.

Mace gathered me in his arms and lifted me up, slipping his hands under my ass as I wrapped my legs around his waist. I could already feel his hard length pressing into me and if he hadn't been holding me I definitely would have collapsed into a puddle on the floor. All I could think about was how incredible and sexy Mace was.

He pressed his lips against mine, so soft and gentle, at first. But it only took a few moments for our kiss to deepen and fireworks went off behind my eyes. He turned and set me on the bed, barely breaking away from our kiss to pull his tee-shirt over his head. I wanted to swoon as I leaned back, enjoying the sight of his broad shoulders, delicious chest with a smattering of hair and those completely ridiculous rippled abs. He was the hottest thing I'd ever laid my eyes on and desire pooled between my legs.

His eyes burned into mine as he popped the top button on his jeans. His voice was a low rumble that sent chills down my spine and shivers up my legs. "I'm not sure how gentle I can be right now, I want you hard and fast and screaming my name."

I crooked one finger at him and all pretensions of being a good girl that made her parents proud skittered out of my head. I wanted my sexy green orc, bad. Seeing him pop another button on his jeans made me whimper and rub my thighs together. I was dripping wet for him already. I licked my lips and said, "I need you, Mace. Right now." My voice sounded husky in my ears. I didn't recognize myself, but I didn't care. I needed him between my legs.

Chapter Twenty-Two

MACE

My cock has never been harder in my life, hearing that husky, sexy voice begging me. The way she was laid back on the bed, she was a buffet—no, a fucking feast. Fuck, I had to taste her again, make sure she was ready for me. I knew that I was on the big side for human women and I wanted her screaming in delight. I knelt on the edge of the bed and grabbed her ankles, spreading them apart to make room for me.

I lifted one leg, making short work of her shoes. One day I'd fuck her up against the wall, while she wore sky high stilettoes, but today, I needed to see her toes curl in ecstasy. Her cute, sensible little flats went flying over my shoulder and I pressed my lips to her ankle. Alexis's skin was soft and smooth and somehow I got even harder as I kissed my way up her leg. I couldn't help but nip at her inner thigh and grinned as her hips rose off the bed and her hands clenched the duvet.

Her skirt slipped to her waist, revealing her glistening folds to me and moaned as I scented her arousal. Fuck, she smelled amazing. I rested her leg on my shoulder and nipped gently at her clit. Her hands buried themselves in my hair and she ground that amazing pussy against my face. It took everything in my power not to plunge into her. I'd never wanted anyone like this, but I had to make sure she was ready for me, I had to make this good for her.

I wanted to explode in her as she screamed my name, but I pushed that urge down and licked her seam from the bottom to the top, then circled the bundle of nerves at the top. I sucked the nub into my mouth and an utterly male satisfaction seared my body as her back arched off the bed. I suckled a moment longer, then thrust my tongue into her waiting core.

It was all I could do to hang on to her as I fucked her with my tongue. Somehow she tasted even more amazing as her arousal soaked my face.

"Oh fuck, Mace, please, I need—" Her voice trailed off as I circled her clit with my fingers, my tongue still deep inside her. "I'm so close!" It came out as a wail and my dick throbbed to be in her. I'd made her come twice on the bus, but that was nothing. I was determined I'd show her exactly what having an orc lover meant. I licked up her seam to her clit and sucked it into my mouth again, slipping a finger into her dripping core.

I lifted my mouth. "Tell me what you need. I want you to beg me for it."

Her lust glazed eyes looked into mine and her tongue darted out and swiped over her lips. A red flush went down her cheeks and disappeared under her shirt. She finally gasped out, "Please Mace, let me come. Make me come on your face."

Her plea went straight to my dick and I dropped my face back to her pussy. I slid another finger into her and curled my fingers until I found the bundle of nerves that marked her g-spot. I took her clit into my mouth again and she mewled in pleasure and I felt her whole body go stiff as she exploded on my hand and face. It was the hottest thing I'd ever seen. I rode the waves with her, milking every ounce of her orgasm until she collapsed against the bed.

I eased my hand out of her and moved to be next to her, gathering her in my arms while her body shuddered with the aftershocks. I watched her face until her eyelids finally fluttered open and she gave me a shy little smile.

She started muttering something about taking care of me and I said, "Lay back baby, I've got you."

She nuzzled into my neck and for the first time in my life, I enjoyed cuddling. My dick was so hard I could pound nails with it, but I wanted to enjoy Alexis. I stroked her glorious mane of hair and down her back. I touched her gently as she came down from her high. It was like I was drunk on her and couldn't stop touching her.

She finally opened her eyes again and said, "But what about you, seriously?"

I didn't say anything but started slowly unbuttoning her shirt, enjoying each inch of creamy flesh that was exposed. I hadn't actually gotten to see her in all her amazing glory and was dying to get my hands on her tits. A sweet little lace bra was exposed. I wasn't sure what style it might be, but her rounded mounds were boosted up and the lace barely covered her nipples. I ran one finger between her breasts, enjoying the feel of her.

I couldn't help myself and gently flicked her still-hard nipple. She moaned softly. I ran my hand down her side to her hip and gently squeezed.

"I can barely move, I've never come like that in my life. I think I'm broken. I think you broke me. Tuck me in."

I laughed and said, "Do you think we're finished? Do you think I'm not going to make you come until you can't remember your name, over and over again tonight?"

Chapter Twenty-Three

ALEXIS

Despite being utterly boneless and spent, his deep chuckle sent another flood of moisture between my legs. I could barely think and was still in a haze after the completely ridiculous orgasm he'd given me. If I thought being sneaky on the bus was hot, that was nothing compared to what he could do with space and time to worship my body.

A shudder racked my body as he squeezed my hip and despite moments ago being certain I had nothing left to give, my pussy throbbed for him. I thought about the amazing cock I'd sucked on the bus and imagined each ridge easing into me. I couldn't help but squirm against him. I'd never had a partner treat me like he did, making my pleasure a priority.

Before I could drift away, I needed to feel his cock in me, I needed to watch him lose himself in my body. It was like I was encased in honey as he slipped my shirt off and eased my skirt down my hips, both items disappearing off the bed.

"Fuck me, your tits are fucking amazing. I need to taste them."

His mouth pushed the scrap of lace out of the way as he suckled on my nipple, his tongue swirling around as desire built up in my body. I clutched his head as sensations shot through me and I ached to feel him between my legs.

"God, please Mace, please."

He lifted his head, his voice thickened and rough. "Tell me what you need, baby. I'll give you everything."

I spread my legs wider, making space for him. A flush rose up from my chest to my cheeks and I said, "I need you, between my legs. In me. I need your cock, Mace."

"Fuck, yes." He eased back and I whimpered, missing his hands on me. "Give me a second, sweetness, I promise I'm not going anywhere."

He shucked his pants and moisture pooled between my thighs. I was going to get to feel that amazing cock in me and I couldn't keep still.

He knelt between my knees and looked down at me, a low rumble of approval in his chest. I stared up at him. His skin was taut over his amazing body and his cock jutted out as he stroked over each delectable ridge.

Goddamn, his cock was fucking beautiful. It was long, thick, and, like the rest of him, a gorgeous shade of green. I wanted him in me, wanted to feel every single ridge ease into me.

He lowered himself over my body and his blunt head brushed against my entrance. He pushed forward and as the head of his cock slid inside my still-throbbing pussy, I gasped and my eyes opened wide. I suddenly wondered if I'd even be able to take a tool this big. But he gasped at the same time, and the sound of his pleasure made me somehow even wetter.

He eased into me so slowly I wanted to die. The stretch almost broke me, it was so intense, but as he moved forward, my body gave in to his. The first ridge slid into me and I had never felt anything so amazing in my life.

I'd never had an orc lover, but had of course, seen pictures, and knew about the ridges. But I couldn't have imagined how amazing it felt as each one stretched me a little further, until finally he was fully seated in me, our bodies pressed together.

But if I thought the ridges were amazing going in? My entire body flexed as he pulled out, far faster than he'd slid in, each and every ridge an otherworldly sensation. Now that my body had stretched to accommodate him, he was able to thrust into me, filling me and each ridge hitting just right. My body was so primed that by the time he bottomed out in me, fireworks exploded behind my eyes and my body clenched around him.

He lightly circled his hips, drawing out my orgasm. "That's right, Alexis, that's my dick you're coming around. And I'm going to make you come over and over again, all night long."

I thought he might give me a moment of respite, but instead he set a furious pace, determined to bring me over the edge. All I could do was wrap my legs around his waist and hold on.

I'd never had anyone make me come so quickly a second time, and definitely not from penetration. But the sensation of those ridges popping in and out of me was more than I could handle and before I knew it, I was keening his name as waves of pleasure washed over me.

"Fuck yeah, your pussy is strangling my cock and I love it. I love every inch of your amazing body."

He grabbed me by my hips, lifted me and flipped me to my knees before I realized what he was doing. I screamed with joy as the ridges hit the backside of my pussy. I'd thought for sure I was done, but that shift sent my body into overdrive. One hand was on my hip as he thrust mercilessly into me and the other circled around, dipping between my legs and his nimble fingers circled my clit.

I was pure sensation, I wasn't sure where I ended and he began. I was awash in an endless wave of pleasure, my pussy contracting around his cock. He pushed me through an endless orgasm. Every time one ended, he'd shift my legs, taking me in a million different ways.

I was somehow building up to another orgasm when he grunted, "Give me one more baby, can you do that? Before I explode in you."

The word gasped out of me, somehow. "Yes, please. Come in me. I want to feel you explode."

The world narrowed even further and all I could focus on was the endless pleasure of him between my legs, his cock pumping in and out of me. My entire body contracted and I was a supernova, screaming his name, shattering beneath him.

"Fuck yes, yes!" As I came, I felt him thicken inside me and my body milked him as he came, filling me to overflowing with his seed, my thighs slick.

We finally slumped on the bed, utterly spent. I could barely move. I'd never come like that before and somehow I doubted I'd ever have sex like that again. There was no way that perfection could be matched.

But instead of falling asleep, Mace shifted my body again and gently stroked me.

"I told you I wasn't even close to being done with you tonight. All night long. I'm going to have you *all night long*."

Chapter Twenty-Four

MACE

I couldn't believe my cock. I mean, I've always been able to fuck a lot. But now, it was unreal. Throughout the night I shot my load all over Alexis' tits, or down her throat, or deep inside her pussy, and all she'd have to do is smile, or touch me, or be near me, and I'd be hard again.

I'd heard about this—orcs being able to fuck for days, coming again and again without ever really losing their erections, but I'd kind of thought it was a legend. I mean, Jax and Clash claimed they did it but I was pretty sure they needed at least twenty minutes to recover, like a normal person.

The only thing that kept me from fucking Alexis every possible second was how much fun she was to talk to. I'd been in relationships before, plenty of them, but I'd never been with anyone I'd liked hanging out with as much.

There'd always been a huge difference between friends and girlfriends. Friends, I talked to and had partied with. Girlfriends, I was romantic with and fucked. Never thought there'd be someone I enjoyed talking about movies and books with who I also wanted to bury my cock in until she screamed.

The morning after the night we spent together, I snuck back to my room super early. I napped for an hour or two, showered, and then messaged Alexis, Shawna, and the band, suggesting we have breakfast in the hotel restaurant.

I wanted to have breakfast with Alexis, and didn't see a way I could finagle it without inviting everyone. Not only would it make my band mates suspicious, if the press got a shot of us having breakfast together, they would immediately assume we must be engaged. The paparazzi could be incredibly relentless, although they tended not to follow us to the smaller cities.

Everyone texted back agreeing. Alexis' text came last and I worried for a while that she was annoyed at me for asking, but once I got the:

sounds good! :-)

I figured she'd been trying to play it cool.

I went down to the hotel restaurant and got the biggest table they had, letting them know how many orcs and how many humans so they'd know what kind of cups and glasses to put on the table. They were cheerful about it, which was nice. It wasn't always like that.

Jax and Clash got there first, then Frey and Torch came down. It seemed like ages before Shawna and Alexis finally arrived. I tried not to look like I was impatient. Finally they walked in and the moment I saw her, both my heart and my cock leapt. She was so beautiful, and so god-damned sexy. She sat down a little gingerly. I was afraid it was going to give us away and I worried that I'd hurt her. But she winked at me before casually looking away.

I'd made sure the orc and human chairs were arranged in such a way that I wouldn't be sitting next to her, because I didn't trust myself. If she was sitting that close to me I probably wouldn't be able to resist touching her, and then the jig would be up. Not that I especially wanted to hide, but Alexis was worried about looking professional.

Unfortunately, it worked out so she was sitting almost directly across from me instead. I tried desperately not to make eye contact, not to look at her at all, because every time I did, her beauty took my breath away. I must have looked like a dumbstruck idiot, but hoped the band was too busy fucking around to pay attention to me eye-banging our manager.

I was relieved when the waitress came to take our orders, giving me something else to concentrate on.

While we waited for the food, I kept my eyes glued to the salt and pepper shakers in the middle of the table, hoping it would look like I was listening intently to whoever was talking. The conversation at first was about the show the night before—it had gone well, except the wrong stage layout had been provided and Alexis blew her top, which was honestly pretty fun to watch.

"It won't happen again," she said now, still looking pretty angry—even though I knew she'd taken a break from thinking about it for most of the night. "I'll be contacting all the other venues today and reconfirming that they understand what they are contractually obligated to provide. And I told the manager last night—if we get to the arena tonight and the equipment still isn't right? We walk."

Everyone's eyebrows rose at this. We'd never had a manager threaten to cancel a show before.

"Will we seriously not play?" Frey asked. "That's not how we usually do things—"

"Yeah, I was mostly bluffing," Alexis admitted with a smile. "But as you know from the other night, I can bluff. I know you'd never want to disappoint your fans. He totally bought it, though. I could see the fear in his eyes." Her phone binged with a text, and her smile faded as she read it.

"He did buy it, right?" Torch asked, a little nervous.

"What? No, he did," Alexis sounded distracted and typed back into the phone for a moment before looking up with a frown. "That wasn't him on the phone, that was one of the record label guys—Jay Overton."

"Jay Overton?" Frey perked up a bit. Of course she perked up, they had some weird secret thing going on. But if she wasn't ready to tell us they were an item, who was I to judge?

Well, I judged a little. Minotaurs were known for their harems and orcs didn't share once they were partnered. I'd hate to have to kill him for breaking Frey's heart. Assuming there was anything left over once Frey was done with him.

"What does he want?" Shawna leaned in to look at the phone over her boss's shoulder.

"Oh, um," Alexis looked around at us as if remembering that we were not friends eating together, but rather a band she was managing. "It was nothing. Just checking in."

"Nope." Frey folded her arms in a way that was half-joking, half-serious. "You checked the phone in front of us, it was a rookie mistake, and now you have to tell us what's up. Is Jay coming to a show or something?"

Alexis looked at our faces—I made mine look as serious as the others, even though when our eyes met I wanted to beam at her and mouth something utterly filthy. For a moment I completely lost track of the conversation and thought about how somehow I hadn't fucked her tits yet.

Chapter Twenty-Five

MACE

"You know, Never Stop didn't demand information like this from me." Alexis' pointed tone brought me back to earth.

"Never Stop was a bunch of thirteen-year-olds," Clash pointed out. "I bet the only questions they asked were all puberty-related."

Alexis laughed at that and I half wanted to punch Clash in the nose as a bit of jealousy burbled up. I wanted to be the one to make Alexis laugh. I was being ridiculous, but I couldn't help but to glower at him.

"Fine," she said, smiling in defeat. "It really isn't anything super important, but I'll tell you. Overton just wants to get on a call later, in order to talk to me about possible changes in the tour schedule."

We all tensed up, and she quickly added, "Nothing major, nothing bad! Possible good news, actually. We have that weird gap in our schedule in a couple weeks. There's a festival and apparently one of the bands has been real squirrelly lately and the organizers aren't sure if they are gonna show up at the festival or be in rehab. The label is considering sending you, if we can make it work."

The whole band groaned as one. I tried not to, since I was willing to be happy about anywhere Alexis sent me as long as she came along. But I couldn't help it. Festivals were awful and I had such bad memories from the last one we'd done. When Aubrey broke my heart and derailed my life.

"What? What's the matter?" Alexis seemed surprised. "I thought this was a good thing?"

We all exchanged glances. I didn't want to be the one to complain, and to my relief Frey spoke first.

"Festivals are the *worst*," she said flatly. "Never enough space, never enough time to set up, and half the time we're playing, we're also keeping an eye on the crowd because you know half the audience is either dehydrated or on who-knows-what."

"Not that we have anything against 'who-knows-what,'" Jax threw in, "We are rock stars, after all."

"Except who would even want to do 'who-knows-what' at a festival?" Clash asked. "For me, 'who-knows-what' is interesting enough—"

Jax cut back in, "Plus, the last festival was not great for Mace—"

"We're getting off-topic," Torch interrupted, much to my relief. "The point is, we would very much appreciate it if you can get us out of doing this festival."

Alexis' face fell. "I'll try," she said, "but I'm not—"

"However," I cut in, "if you can't get us out of it, we will of course be completely professional about it, as we understand that festivals are part of being a band on tour, which we are lucky to be." I glared around at the others, and they quickly chimed in with agreement. I didn't want to have to explain to Alexis how the whole Aubrey situation had gone down at our last festival.

"It's not that we won't do it," Frey said. "We'd just like to complain about it a lot." She brightened. "But you guys get to complain with us! You'll probably hate it at least as much as we do."

Shawna and Alexis both laughed. "That IS a bright side," Alexis said. "I don't know if I can get us out of it, but at the least I swear I won't move heaven and earth to make it happen. Will that work? Overton was pretty aggressive about what a great opportunity it was to fill in a gap in our schedule."

Was Alexis saying "us" instead of "you" calculated, to make it seem like we were all part of the same team or whatever? I definitely didn't care. I really liked her saying "us" like that. I liked us being on a team, working together.

Torch was laughing, but in a friendly way. "Overton doesn't want to pay for hotels while we're sitting around and waiting for the next show. It's always money with those guys." I caught Frey giving him major side-eye over that comment, but the conversation swirled around us and I let it go. Let Frey have her little secrets.

The topic turned as we finished breakfast, with all of us sharing our worst show stories. Frey talked about the time she sat down at her drum set, picked up her sticks, and at the very first tap of stick on drum, the entire set collapsed around her. Turned out later that a disgruntled roadie had removed all the screws after she wouldn't, well, screw him.

Then Jax and Clash shared about the show where they got a note from some cute groupies to meet them at an all-night restaurant around the corner from the hotel, but when they got there and saw them in the fluorescent lights, the girls were clearly not a day over fifteen.

"What did you do?" Shawna asked, leaning forward, her eyes wide.

"What do you think we did?" Jax snorted. "We hid in the bathroom and called Frey to come get us. Frey ended up sitting with them until their parents showed up to drive them home. So they did get to hang out with a rock star, at least."

Everyone laughed. It hadn't seemed all that funny at the time, but now it was hilarious to remember how completely freaked out the twins were.

"Now you," Torch said to Alexis and Shawna. "You must have some good stories." I knew he was probably trying to get out of telling one, but since my worst show story was something I most definitely did not want to talk about, I kept my trap shut. Plus, when Alexis was talking it gave me an excuse to look at her.

"Touring with kids leads to very different stories than tours with regular bands," Alexis said. "They all have an adult with them, usually a parent or an aunt or uncle. So most of our stories have to do with boring arguments with their guardians. PTA stuff. Oh, and threats to cancel shows if they didn't do their homework."

"We considered it our duty," Shawna put in, "to make sure the kids didn't turn into entitled dicks. We did our best. It's really hard not to get a swelled head when you're thirteen and the world is telling you how amazing you are." She turned and gave Alexis a look. "There is one story that isn't boring, Alexis. Not boring at all. And it's how we got this job!"

Alexis flushed. It was adorable. "I don't think that's really the sort of story they want to hear, and we're not supposed to talk about it yet—"

"Oh, come on," Shawna urged her. "If you don't tell them, I will! I trust them to keep it secret!"

Indecision showed on Alexis' face, but she finally made her mind up and nodded firmly at us. "Okay, fine," she said with a laugh, "but pinky swear, you guys: until the press embargo is up, no talking about it."

As one, we put our pinkies out and said, "Pinky swear!"

Chapter Twenty-Six

Mace

Alexis looked up at the ceiling for a moment, then sighed and began to speak as if she was reciting a story she'd memorized. "It was right before the last show of the tour. We were all set to go on the shuttle bus from the airport to the next venue, when a new guy from the record label called. They'd scheduled a special luncheon for the parents and guardians, to thank them for everything."

Shawna interjected, "The plan was that when the plane landed, the shuttle bus would drop all the adults off at this restaurant, and take the boys on to the venue with our driver and one of the assistants watching over them. It was all normal enough—the record label did this sort of thing sometimes, and the bus driver could get the kids where they needed to go. No big deal, right?"

"Besides," Alexis said, "Shawna had gone to the venue ahead of us, because we'd gotten a call saying there was a problem with some merchandise, and she was in charge of that. So she'd be there to collect the kids when they arrived."

She turned and looked at Shawna. "Maybe if you'd been with us, that day, you would have realized something was wrong."

Shawna shook her head. "No one realized, Alexis. There's no reason to think I would have."

Alexis nodded and continued. "So, we got off the bus at the restaurant, waved goodbye to the kids, and went inside, where we were told there was no reservation for us. They didn't have a clue what we were talking about.

"So at first we figured there'd been a mix-up with restaurants. I got the record label on the phone. And they didn't know what we were talking about either." Alexis closed her eyes, clearly reliving the moment. "I didn't want the parents to panic, so I got them a table and told them I needed to make some phone calls, figure things out." Alexis looked a little pale.

"I was about to call Shawna, to make sure the boys had arrived safely, when the phone rang. It was our bus driver." Her voice became flinty. "Our bus driver, who'd been driving us around for months, who we thought was our friend, for god's sake, telling me that he had the boys. He and the assistant were holding them, and wanted 20 million dollars to give them back. He said we had six hours, at which point he'd—" She swallowed and went even paler. "At which point he'd start cutting off fingers."

Shawna reached over and took Alexis' hand while we all gasped, even though it had been pretty clear where this was going.

"It was that bit that did it," she said. "That and the fact that I could hear crying in the background. The thing about these boys—" She paused, searching for words. "They're special. They are, in a weird way, seriously disadvantaged. They've been performing since they were little, studying dance and music full time. A lot of them have never been to regular school. One of them—I'm not saying who but it was one of the humans—didn't know how to read until I became their manager and insisted he learn. They have no survival skills whatsoever. They've never needed any, because they've been surrounded by adults doing everything for them, telling them they're amazing.

"They're not bad kids, they're very sweet and all, but they don't know how to handle the tiniest bit of adversity. Like, if their shoelace breaks they freeze and wait for someone to bring them a new shoelace. And they get their feelings hurt so fast, it makes you want to hug them all the time. So hearing them wailing and the fear in their voices? Hearing this guy saying he was going to cut off their fingers, I went—" She broke off again. "Oh, wait. Do you all know I'm a witch? This won't make a lot of sense if you don't."

Frey and I both nodded. Torch, Jax, and Clash were all surprised. "How come we've never seen you do any magic?" Jax asked. I wanted to kick him for interrupting when I was dying to know what had happened next.

"'Cause I don't do much magic," Alexis said with a shrug. "I'm not particularly powerful, and it doesn't come up much. I use it for mending and stuff like that, but nothing big."

"Usually nothing big," Shawna corrected, and Alexis smiled.

"Right, usually nothing big. But strong emotions, like fear or anger or panic or"—she glanced at me, then quickly looked away—"things like that, can make witches a lot more powerful than we usually are.

So when this asshole said he was going to hurt my boys, when I knew he probably already had hurt them some, I went—" Her eyes clouded. "Berserk, I guess, is a good word for it. I became powerful in a way I'd never imagined. I had enough of a connection with the boys that I could feel in the very marrow of my bones where they were. The pull of them called out to me with a sound like an air raid siren. While I'm not normally a flier, this time, I didn't even think about it. I rose in the air and rocketed towards this little building on the edge of town."

Alexis sat back and took a sip of water.

Frey leaned forward and said, "Girl, please, do not leave us hanging like that. What happened next?"

She wrinkled her eyes and looked a little embarrassed. "And, well, I tore the roof off of it. I sort of threw it to the side. I found out later that it didn't land on anything important but honestly that was pure luck. I was absolutely enraged and not thinking very clearly.

"The boys were huddled together against a wall, bound up with rope and with duct tape over their mouths, and two men with guns plus our bus driver standing over them, and—" She stopped, looking a little helpless. "I actually don't remember the next bit very well."

"That's okay," Shawna cut in eagerly, her words tumbling out in a rush. "The boys told me later. She was flying and there was all this electricity crackling around her and she pointed at the men and snakes of electricity wrapped around all three of them and they were flung against the wall and their guns cracked in half and there was a sort of silver magical cage around them, and then Alexis landed and walked to the boys and the rope and tape melted away and they were lifted and surrounded by velvet air—well they all described it a little differently but eventually settled on velvet air—and then all their bruises and cuts from when the bad guys worked them over disappeared, and Alexis was like ten feet tall—"

Alexis threw up her hands and interrupted. "And the boys were thirteen, so if there's one thing we know for sure, they exaggerated all this," she finished. "But, yeah, the kidnappers were incapacitated and the boys were fine. I called the police and the record label in quick succession, and the parents didn't even know anything had happened until the cops showed up at the restaurant to tell them everything was okay. And I went back to not being very powerful."

I was staring at Alexis with my mouth open. We all were, although I didn't think they were feeling like their hearts were going to burst like I did. I was in awe of this woman, this beautiful strong woman who was telling this incredible story of her own heroism like it was no big deal. I wanted to lunge across the table and kiss her. The only thing that kept me back was knowing she wouldn't like me to do it in front of everyone.

Chapter Twenty-Seven

MACE

Frey was the first of us to speak. "How," she breathed, "have we not heard about this? How was it not in all the papers?"

Alexis shrugged. "Keeping it out of the papers was the number-one priority once the kids were safe. The record label has to control the narrative, you know."

"The big outlets agreed to a press embargo in exchange for some exclusive interviews. You guys, you know how that goes. The band will go on a talk show in a month or two, but right now, they're all in therapy dealing with PTSD. It was very scary, especially for children who'd basically never been scared before. They'll tell their story, and it will be the talk of the town for a day or two, and it'll probably make their next record go platinum."

"But what about you?" Torch asked, sounding a little angry, which was a feeling I mirrored. "You're a hero! You should be covered in medals, or something!"

Alexis shook her head. "It's the last thing I want. Like I told you, I am not usually very powerful. Once people think you can fly and shoot electricity out of your hands, that's all they want you to do. Anyway, I did get something. I got promoted to managing you lot."

She smiled, and I suddenly felt very glad she didn't want medals.

Shawna nudged her. "You did not get the promotion for doing magic." She turned to us. "The record was pretty happy she rescued them, of course. But she got the promotion because of how she handled the aftermath. Keeping it out of the papers, keeping the label from being sued by the parents, convincing the public that the stomach flu that caused the show to be canceled was the puking kind, not the pooping kind—"

The band all laughed and Alexis poked her. "That last bit was all you!"

"It was!' Shawna admitted. "The trick is telling a gross story about puking, and that makes people think they've heard everything gross there is to hear."

"So how come you didn't get a promotion too," Torch asked, grinning at her.

Alexis rolled her eyes at Shawna. "Yeah, how come?" she asked wryly.

Shawna rolled her eyes too. "They offered me one. They wanted me to take over managing Never Stop on their next tour. But given the choice between running around after a bunch of tweeners, and touring with my favorite band while working with the best boss I've ever had? I chose the latter. Sue me for wanting to like my job. I wanted to be involved with rock-and-roll, so this felt like a better move for me."

There was a brief pause. Then Jax said, "We're your faaaaaa-vorite?"

Shawna snorted. "I meant favorite genre."

"No, you can't take it back," Clash said. "You loooooovvvve us!"

As the rest of the table laughed and joked, I still gazed at Alexis with awe. What an amazing woman, so capable and competent. And when motivated by love—mind-bogglingly powerful. That she was so moved to protect the children in her care gave me a weird ache in my chest. She probably didn't even realize how incredibly important family and taking care of children is to orcs. But that she risked herself was a little terrifying and extremely sexy.

She looked at me, our gazes locked on to each other, and my now rock-hard cock shifted in my pants.

"Well," I said, "I should get back to my room and get things ready for the show."

Alexis nodded. "I have tons of work to do. Shall we settle up?"

We paid the bill as quickly as possible, then headed upstairs. So that no one would suspect anything, I headed for the staircase while she took the elevator. I took the stairs four at a time and arrived at my room at the same moment she did. Luckily the rest of the band and Shawna weren't lurking in the hallway, but I don't think I would have much cared if they were.

I unlocked the door, pulled her inside, and grabbed the front of her dress. "So being a witch means if I tear this, you can mend it, right?"

She licked her lips and nodded slowly at me. I grabbed the front of her dress and flexed, completely shredding it. Scraps of fabric fluttered to the ground around her feet. Fuck, she was so hot in her lacy little bra and blood rushed south when I realized she'd done as I asked, and wasn't wearing any underwear. I hoisted her up and Alexis wrapped her legs around my waist.

I could feel the heat of her pressed against my cock and I staggered to the bed. Even after taking her all night long, my hard-on raged like a horny teenager's.

"I'm going to fuck you till neither one of us can move."

She leaned back and spread her legs, then held up her hand, reaching with the other for her phone.

"I'll set a timer," she said, "so we don't miss the show."

"If I had my way, I'd fuck you all the way to the bus and then onto the stage."

She giggled at me, but I was half serious. Being near her made me hard as steel and all I could think about was sinking into her waiting warmth.

We collided on the bed and I set out to prove exactly how much I wanted her.

Chapter Twenty-Eight

*A*LEXIS

We collapsed next to each other. Judging by the rigidness of his giant member, he could have gone again, but I needed a break. And his panting indicated that he did too, hard cock or not.

He crooked his arm and pulled me to him, my head against his warm chest. "I've been thinking," he said. "What if I quit the band and you quit your job, and we stay in this room forever, fucking?"

"It's a nice idea," I mused. My fingers traced his tight abs. "But then I wouldn't get to see you be a rock star. That's like, 50% of why I'm into you. Oh, and the other 50% is how good you are at doing crosswords on the bus." I wiggled against him a little so he'd know this wasn't true. Well, the crossword puzzle bit kind of was.

"Fine," he chuckled and kissed the top of my head. "But I'll tell you what. Tonight, I'm going to sing every single song for you. It might look like I'm singing them to the audience, but I'm only singing to you."

I pulled back and looked at him, my nose wrinkling. "Seriously?" I asked.

His eyebrows raised, surprised. "What? I thought that was, like, over-the-top romantic."

My eyebrows were raised too. "Again: seriously? Have you ever listened to your songs? Your number-one hit is "Blood Beating," off the album *Gallons of Gore*.

"Right, that's right," he nodded thoughtfully. "We're an Orc Rock band, I forgot. Surely we have at least one ballad?"

"You all are known for *never* doing ballads. You said in an interview recently that you would sooner switch to only doing Celine Dion covers than do a ballad. Which made no sense, because all her songs are ballads."

"Yeah, well," Mace said. "I secretly like Celine Dion. She's my mother's favorite." He grinned. "You read my interviews?"

"Yeah, I have to, I'm your tour manager, remember?"

"Sure, that's why." He pulled me on top of him, his hard cock digging into my stomach and making me think maybe my break was over. I moved so that the tip was brushing against the lips of my pussy, and his eyes lit up. I was so fucking wet for him.

"Tell you what," he said, placing his hands on my shoulders. "You tell me what interview is your favorite, while I gently—" He began pushing on my shoulders, causing me to sink down

HIS ROCK HARD RHYTHM

onto his cock. As it filled me to bursting, all thoughts of interviews left my head.

"Ohhhhhh" I moaned.

"Yeah," he said. "That's my favorite too."

Chapter Twenty-Nine

Several Weeks Later
ALEXIS

After many more nights on tour, more rounds of glorious, orgasm-filled afternoons, more evenings full of rock-and-roll hijinks, I got a text that made me remember what anxiety felt like. Suddenly all I could do was worry about finally meeting with the record label guy in person.

Shawna watched me sympathetically as I paced the green room. "It's not like you're in trouble or anything," she pointed out. "Overton just wants to talk in person about the festival, since we head there tomorrow morning. Dude probably wanted a ride on the label's private jet."

"I know, I know," I said, "but still. It's my first in-person meeting with the label since we took this job. We've only been on the road for a few weeks. If I'm doing anything wrong, I'm about to find out. Also, why isn't he here yet? He was supposed to arrive before the show started, and they're halfway through the first set."

At that very moment, my phone buzzed in my pocket. Pulling it out, I saw a text from Jay Overton that read:

> *Plane landed but running late. Will get to the venue after the show, or possibly meet you at the hotel bar.*

I rolled my eyes. "He's in town but 'running late.' I think you were right, by the way. He's probably having a fancy dinner somewhere on the expense account."

"He's probably too lame to like Orc Rock, so he wants to miss the show," Shawna sneered. "He's probably secretly a Never Stop fanboy."

I laughed and she jumped to her feet. "You know what this means, right?" She grabbed my hand and pulled me towards the door. "We can go listen to the show with the rest of the audience."

"We can listen," I said. "But not from the audience! I've told you before, we stand on the side of the stage like professionals." But I picked up speed as we went down the hall, until I was almost running. I couldn't wait to watch Mace perform, to make music, to do his favorite thing in the world. Well, maybe second favorite. First might be that thing he liked to do with his tongue.

When the show was over, I popped back to the green room to see if Overton was there, but it was empty. Hotel bar it was, then. I wandered back into the hallway, thinking I'd head outside and catch a cab, since the others probably wouldn't be ready to leave for at least another hour or so.

As I walked towards the elevator that would take me to the street, a familiar scent hit me and then strong arms encircled me from behind. Instantly my whole body was tingling, my pussy wet.

"I have to talk to you right away," Mace growled in my ear. "It's kind of an emergency."

I quickly—if reluctantly—squirmed out of his embrace, and looked around to see if we'd been spotted. The corridor was blessedly empty, but I whispered my next words anyway. "Mace!" I hissed, "be cool! You know I need to keep this quiet."

His eyes flashed, more amused than chastised. He looked around quickly, then opened the nearest door. "In here, then," he said.

It was a storage room, barely bigger than a closet, filled with old chairs and tech equipment. "Fine." I stepped inside and closed the door behind us, my pulse racing. We shouldn't be doing this, but I couldn't stop myself from touching Mace.

He took my face in his hands and kissed me, and for a moment I melted against him. But then I pushed him gently away. "I have to go talk to the record label exec, remember?" I said. "He's probably at the hotel now." But I rubbed his cock through his pants. Fuck, he was so hard already.

"Surely he can wait. This is urgent." He unzipped his pants and his giant member sprang free. My knees started to buckle and all I wanted to do was fall to my knees and take him into my mouth. To make him come down my throat, losing himself completely. With great effort, however, I managed to stay on my feet.

"I'm sorry," I said firmly. "I really can't. I have to do my job now. Put that thing away and I'll take care of it later tonight."

He cocked his head, tucking himself back into his pants. "Then maybe I could eat your pussy for a while, to get you nice and relaxed for the meeting? I promise I won't keep you long. Three or four orgasms, tops."

He stuck out his long tongue and licked the tip of one tusk, and I was lost. Mace dropped to his knees in front of me and pushed my skirt up to my waist. I grabbed his hair, trying to stifle a moan as he pressed his face against the apex of my thighs

He was so strong and I didn't have it in me to resist as he put one of my legs over his shoulder, splitting me wide open for his mouth. He lifted me into the air and settled me on his face, his arms between my legs, hands firm on my ass.

All I could do was hang on as he tongue-fucked me into an orgasm. I lost all sense of time and place and I shuddered as I dangled in the air, my pussy pressed against him.

Mace slowly lowered me down and my knees almost buckled as my feet hit the floor. He steadied me and chuckled.

"Fuck, you are goddamn delicious. I love having you ride my face. That's definitely something to repeat." He leaned forward and stroked my dripping center with two fingers, before plunging them into me. "I need your cunt so fucking bad."

His thumb circled my clit as I rode his hand. It was hard to form thoughts. "Mace, fuck, you need to stop. I have to message Overton."

"But wouldn't it be so much better, if instead of stopping, you got on your hands and knees and I pounded you while you sent your text?"

My brain stuttered as I imagined him grabbing me by the hair and fucking me, hard and rough. The image of him made me come on his hand. Our eyes locked on each other as he slid his hand out of my pussy and licked his fingers clean.

I almost relented. But I steeled myself against temptation, even as my quivering pussy protested. I staggered but I pulled my skirt down, hiding the evidence of my lust on my thighs. I'd need to find a bathroom to clean-up in before I ran into anyone.

"Sorry," I said, giving him one last kiss. "It's time for professional Alexis. I swear I'll be slutty, cock-hungry Alexis again soon. Give me a few hours to get this meeting done. Especially if you want me to get you out of the festival."

I opened the door and stepped into the hall, straightening my skirt as I did—and almost walked straight into the slab of beef that was Jay Overton.

The record label representative had apparently decided to come to the venue after all.

Chapter Thirty

*A*LEXIS

"Alexis!" he lifted one eyebrow, a confused smile on his face. His eyes darted from me to Mace and back. "Glad to run into you." He glanced into the room behind us, and somehow his eyebrow lifted even higher. It was clearly not a room we had any reason to be in. Oh fuck me, we were straight-up busted by the boss.

"Mr. Overton," I said, my mind racing as I clenched my thighs together, trying not to think about how I'd just been riding Mace's face. How Mace's face was probably still shiny. *Fuck.*

He interrupted me, "It's just Jay; we're colleagues. Besides, when you say 'Mr. Overton', I look for my sire."

"Jay. Have you met Mace, AxeBender's lead singer? I mean, of course you have. You signed him to the label, obviously. I mean, he signed on to your label. I mean—" I was babbling. This was not good.

"Good to see you, man. It's been a while since you hopped on tour." Mace reached past me to shake Overton's hand, his voice friendly and relaxed. He, apparently, did not think this was a big deal.

"We were—" my brain began to catch up. "Discussing a problem Mace is having with one of the roadies. Naturally we didn't want to be overheard." The excuse sounded dumb even as I said it. We had clearly been canoodling. Were my witch powers strong enough that I could literally sink into the ground?

"I see." Overton looked back and forth between us, a slight grin on his face. To my horror, I felt Mace's hand cup my ass. Did he think this was some sort of joke?

Even if Overton couldn't see, which was likely the case, Mace clearly didn't think it was a problem that my professional reputation was in danger of being ruined. If anyone else walked down the hall, they would see Mace's hand firmly gripping my ass, and with the way rumors flew, I'd be lucky if it took fifteen minutes for the news to get around the whole crew.

I stepped forward, away from Mace's stupid hand, and took Overton's arm. "The green room is this way," I said. "We can sit and talk there."

As we walked, Mace fell into step beside us. I shot him a glare and said in my friendliest, most professional voice, "Mace, you will, of course, want to go to your dressing room. I'll address our little issue later."

There was a hurt and confused look on his face, but I didn't care. He'd obviously never had a real job, with a real boss who could really fire him, or at least demote him to the point he might as well quit.

I mean, I knew he never had. The only "job" he'd ever had was dancing around on a stage singing stupid songs. He didn't care if he put my job in jeopardy. I was being a little harsh, maybe, but he didn't seem to understand that he could get me *fired*.

I strode down the hall with Overton, refusing to look and see if Mace was following or not.

The meeting didn't last long. He basically handed me an updated schedule and a folder with more information about the festival. I was a little surprised he'd bothered to fly in for it. It was the epitome of "this could have been an email." He rode back with me to the hotel, but turned down my invitation to get a drink in the bar.

I was relieved. All I wanted was to be alone, and I headed to my room, grateful when I didn't run into anybody. I put the *Do Not Disturb* sign on my door and tried to concentrate on the info packet about the festival I had not managed to get them out of.

The headlining band was Orkestra, the biggest Orc Rock band out there, but AxeBender would be the second in the lineup. Something about Orkestra was tickling my brain, something I should be remembering. The only thing that came to mind was the record label trying to poach them from their current label, and I decided that must be it.

The *Do Not Disturb* sign on the door did not stop Mace from knocking, a little while later. He'd also sent several texts, which was maddening because he sent them when I was still in the meeting with Overton. I'd claimed it was a family text chain and turned my phone to silent.

When Mace knocked at the door, I finally texted him back.

> *I am tired and am not currently on the clock. If there is any tour manager business I need to attend to, you may let Shawna know and I will attend to it in the morning.*

Seconds later my phone binged, and I read his latest text:

> *Alexis, please. Why are you being like this? Talk to me.*

I took a deep breath. He didn't get it. Unbelievable. I almost sent the same text again, but instead typed out:

You did not listen when I told you I needed to work. You threatened both my job and my reputation with your behavior. You behaved in a way that shows plainly you do not respect me.

I hit send, and then typed again.

> *It is also my fault. It was deeply inappropriate for me to become involved with a member of a band I am managing. I hope we can have a proper, professional relationship in future.*

My eyes burned with unshed tears and I didn't realize I was holding my breath until I got the return text. I reluctantly looked at it. It simply said:

Sorry.

I heard his heavy footsteps as he moved away from the door.

Then I put my phone on silent, lay down on the bed, and bawled my eyes out. I was angry at myself for being unprofessional, angry at him for treating me with disrespect, and, most of all, disappointed that he hadn't knocked the door down to get me anyways.

Chapter Thirty-One

MACE

I didn't get it.

Maybe I should have, but I didn't. We'd been having such a great time, and of course I respected her work. I didn't know the record guy was going to be there. Alexis had said he was going to the hotel. And yes, okay, I'd put my hand on her ass while she was talking to him, but I was being funny. I was certain there was no way he could have seen it. And I knew why he really flew in. He was certainly in no position to give us any grief.

I know orcs and humans are a little different when it comes to sex stuff, they're a lot more uptight, basically, but even so I couldn't figure out what had gone so terribly awry.

Once in my room, I paced for hours. I couldn't quiet my brain, trying to figure out what I had done wrong, and what I could do to fix it. What I wanted to do was go back to her room and make her let me in.

My berserker orc brain wanted to kick in the door, throw her over my shoulder and eat her pussy until she wasn't mad anymore. But I figured if she was upset with me for being disrespectful, I probably wouldn't make her feel better by disrespecting her request that I leave her alone.

Maybe Frey would know what to do. I walked down the hall towards her room and loud music reverberated down the hallway, and after a moment of confusion I remembered that the rest of the band were having a party. They'd mentioned it, but I'd said I was too tired to come. At the time, I just thought it would mean no one would notice when I snuck off to be with Alexis.

I almost turned around and went back to my room, but Jax burst into the hall and caught sight of me. "MACE!" he yelled, obviously already ridiculously drunk.

"Hey, Jax," I sighed. "Frey in there?"

"No, she went to her room," he slurred. "She's so boring, Mace! Now I have no one to drink with. Well, except for—" he waved an arm at the room full of people. "But I don't want them. Come drink with me, Mace!"

He held out a large bottle of blordrot and I decided that maybe this was exactly what I needed. I took the bottle from his hand, gulped it all down, and went into the party to find more. As I went, I threw the empty bottle back over my shoulder, delighting in the sound of it smashing against the hallway wall. I felt the familiar jump in my veins, something I usually only felt on stage. My muscles tensed and the echoes of ancient battle cries rang in my head. This was a good night for a rampage.

I snapped awake as the cold water hit my face, and leapt up with a shout.

Shawna stood in front of me. She didn't flinch at my roaring and stared at me stonily. "We should have left half an hour ago," she said. "Clean yourself up, grab your things, and get your ass on the bus."

She turned and walked out of the room, and I shook my head, trying to clear it. What the hell had happened? How much had I had to drink?

I remembered the half-bottle I'd taken from Jax, and then going into the party and drinking a few more bottles, which was a lot for me, and then—*oh god*. I didn't remember much, but I definitely remembered smashing the window and throwing crap into the pool.

I looked down at my hands. There were large splinters of wood stuck in them, luckily fairly shallow so I couldn't feel it. I pulled one out and examined it. I couldn't be sure, but it seemed pretty likely I'd smashed up something with my bare hands. A chair, maybe a desk.

Remembering what Shawna had said, I ran through the shower and threw stuff into my suitcases. When I picked up my phone, I had 47 missed texts. My heart leapt, thinking maybe Alexis had texted, but she hadn't.

The texts were all from the band, congratulating me on my bad behavior, and from Shawna, wondering angrily where the hell I was. Oh, and a slew of news alerts. I didn't read the articles but the headlines screamed:

BAD ORCS OF ROCK AT IT AGAIN! HOTEL TRASHED! TOUR CANCELED?

Whatever. The fans loved it. Even if we'd kind of promised we weren't going to behave quite so badly again. I grimaced. Alexis was going to be so, incredibly, epically pissed.

I made my way downstairs. My bandmates were huddled at the bus door, everyone but Frey looking as bad as I felt. Shawna came out and handed us cups of coffee the size of buckets, looking more resigned than friendly.

"Let's go," she said, and we all dutifully found seats. We sat close to one another, not out of affection so much as the need to be near the bathroom in case we puked.

Shawna climbed on the bus after us, spoke to the driver, and he closed the door and began to pull out of the parking lot. I looked around, my heart suddenly racing. "Wait," I called, "What about Alexis? Where is she?"

Shawna made her way down the aisle and glared at me. "Alexis," she said, "is still at the hotel, begging them to forgive us and not sue. She and Jay Overton will catch up with us later.

I, meanwhile, will spend the next seven hours trying to find a hotel that will give us rooms—every single one we had booked for the rest of the tour canceled the second the tabloids posted videos. If I can't find a place for you guys, I think the rest of the tour will be canceled."

She shook her head, now looking sad. "We told you. We told you not to do this. What the absolute fuck got into you last night?" She started to turn away, then remembered something. "I emailed you all the info on the festival. Be sure to read it at some point before we get there this afternoon."

She went back to the front of the bus and opened her laptop. We all sat in miserable silence, not looking at one another. Frey hadn't even been there, but looked guilty as well. Probably because she knew that if she had been there, she would have gone just as far as us—Freya loves a good rampage too.

Finally Torch groaned and stood. "I'm going to go apologize to Shawna," he said.

"I should do it," I protested. "I don't remember much, but I'm pretty sure I started it last night."

"Oh, you definitely did," Torch agreed. "But let me. You look like you're still drunk. Get some more sleep, man."

He stood up and walked towards the front, holding tight to the backs of the seats for balance. He was in better condition than me, maybe, but he clearly wasn't feeling great either.

I decided to take his advice. What I really wanted to do was text Alexis, but that didn't seem like a good idea. I would talk to her when we caught up at the hotel.

I leaned back in the seat, closed my eyes, and let the motion of the bus rock me to sleep.

Chapter Thirty-Two

MACE

I woke hours later to the sound of Frey swearing, softly but furiously. "What is it?" I asked, sitting up. She was staring at her phone like it had punched her.

As soon as I spoke, she put the phone down. "Nothing," she told me. "I just—got an email that some stock I'd bought last week had crashed."

"Okay." I didn't care much. "I'm gonna get something to eat." I stood and walked to the front of the bus where the fridge was, right behind Shawna. Torch was still sitting there, but as I approached I heard his phone bing, and a moment later he stood up and pushed past me, headed to the back of the bus.

I figured his hangover had finally caught up with him. I grabbed a giant-sized energy drink and some beef sandwiches, and got a bottle of water for Torch in case he had, as I suspected, gone to throw up.

But as I headed back, I saw he wasn't in the bathroom. He was sitting next to Frey. Jax and Clash had swiveled in their seats to face them, and they were all whispering furiously. When I approached their heads snapped up to stare at me.

"What is it?" I asked. They didn't say anything. I opened the energy drink and began to swig it down. "Seriously, what?" I asked again, starting to get annoyed.

Finally Torch cleared his throat and spoke. "Hey, so, no big deal," he said. "But we found out who the headlining band at the festival is."

"So it's not us?" I frowned. "That kind of sucks, but it's not too surprising. We were just added to the lineup. What's the big deal?"

Torch shook his head. "It's not that, it's—"

Jax rolled his eyes. "The headlining band is Orkestra."

I stared at them, the blood rushing in my ears. My jaw clenched, my heart was pounding, and my hand *hurt*.

It struck me that it was weird that my hand hurt, so I looked down. I'd crushed the energy drink can so ferociously that the metal cut into my fingers, deep enough for me to feel it. With great effort, I opened my fist.

"Okay," I said. "That's okay. It's fine. I'm going to go back to sleep for a while."

I turned away and went to a seat farther from them, grateful that they knew me well enough to not follow. I pulled my hoodie up and leaned my head against the window.

Aubrey. I was going to see Aubrey.

Fucking *Aubrey*.

I met Aubrey at the beginning of our last tour. She was in the green room one night, technically a groupie, but not like other groupies. Aubrey was special. We were inseparable from that first night on. She rode on the bus with me and slept in my room. I'd had girlfriends but never anyone like her.

She was so far out of my league, so smart and sophisticated. She was super jealous, and I admit it, I was flattered. Whenever I so much as spoke to a groupie she'd get mad and walk off. I'd have to run after her and apologize, then we'd have a screaming fight that would end in the most amazing sex. In retrospect, it was wildly toxic and unhealthy—but at the time, I was completely ensnared.

I was certain that she was all I needed in the world. I was ready to marry her and have kids with her and do pretty much whatever she wanted. I dreamt of her every night and thought about her all day, every day. I believed she made everything about life better.

She was really helpful. She helped rewrite our setlists and arranged for me to be interviewed in a bunch of magazines that got us killer press. She remade my stage look. She insisted we get better snacks in the green room. I couldn't figure out why the rest of the band always seemed so annoyed with her. I thought everything she did was perfect.

Because I was a lovestruck idiot.

Until she met the lead singer of Orkestra, "Lewd," which is a dumb name. It was like I'd never meant anything to her at all.

We were at a week-long festival and I'm pretty sure she started cheating on me that first night, and got more and more obvious about it. I tried to tell myself I was imagining it, that she'd never do something like that. Not to me.

Finally, the last night of the festival, she went to take a nap and I asked Torch and Frey if they thought she was being weird. Torch said he kind of thought so, maybe, yeah, but Frey said, "Only if you think fucking around on you is weird."

I said it wasn't true and Torch chimed in that it was, and I got angrier than I've ever been and said some really nasty things that I would give anything to take back. I stormed off to find Aubrey.

I was going to ask her to marry me and tell her I was quitting the band, which she'd been trying to get me to do for ages. She'd said they were holding me back and were jealous of our relationship. In that moment, after they'd told me all those terrible lies about her cheating, I knew right then she'd been right about the band all along.

So I went to find her. I walked into my dressing room, *my own dressing room,* there was Aubrey except she wasn't alone and she wasn't *napping* before the show.

She was in the reverse cowgirl position, mounted on Lewd's dick.

Chapter Thirty-Three

MACE

She and I ended up having a screaming fight outside in the rain, which actually wasn't that unusual for us. This time it was different. She told me it was over, that she was in love with Lewd.

Instead of being super cool and awesome and telling her I didn't care, like a good rock star, I begged her not to leave me. But she left me, and laughed as she walked away. The rest of the band came and got me later—I was still out there, having what Frey calls a temper tantrum and I call a loud and angry discussion with the gods—and took me back to my room.

Luckily the tour was almost over. I played the last couple shows on autopilot. The day after it ended, my mom and Frey's mom showed up at the hotel and informed me that I wasn't going home, I was going to a special place for people who were having emotional breakdowns.

You'd think it would have been humiliating, having them make this kind of decision for me, but honestly I was really happy to have someone tell me what to do, when I was feeling so unbelievably lost.

I said goodbye to my friends and asked them to forgive me for not believing them and for being such a dick.

They said they forgave me and Jax added, "'Aubrey and Lewd'? More like 'Farty and Pooed.'" That stupid little joke made me feel better than made any real sense. My therapist told me later that it was a reassurance that my world still existed.

So I went to this place in the desert. They call it a spa but it's more like rehab for people whose issues aren't with drugs and alcohol but with people or other emotional stuff.

Lots of time sitting in groups talking. Lots of long walks and exercise. Lots and lots of therapy, basically. By the end of it, I felt a lot better. I had put too much of my identity into Aubrey, had let her consume me so that I didn't know who I was anymore.

Being in that place helped me remember. I wrote a lot of songs there, more songs than I ever would have thought I could write in a couple months.

Of course most of them weren't any good. A few of them were me screaming her name a bunch. But some were great and we ended up using four of them on the new album. None of the ones we used were about Aubrey, at least not so you'd know.

"Chicken Liver Heart" came closest, but if anyone asks I say it's about the time I ate a live chicken, which obviously never happened, but the fans like the story and the song.

But, even though I felt a lot better, I didn't have any interest in meeting anyone new. Or even fucking anyone new. No interest at all. Until Alexis. Alexis swept all memories of Aubrey away.

Being with Alexis was a revelation. I hadn't known I could want to fuck someone while also wanting to be friends with them. That romance and passion didn't have to involve jealousy and pain. With Alexis it was easy and fun—

And now Alexis had dumped me. And I was about to see Aubrey and Lewd. I closed my eyes and leaned my head back against the seat.

"More like 'Farty and Pooed,'" I thought. "More like 'Farty and Pooed.'" Once again, remembering the stupid joke helped.

No matter what, my band would be with me, making stupid-ass jokes.

Chapter Thirty-Four

ALEXIS

When things are bad, the best thing to do is work hard. So in a way it was good that instead of waking up and spending the morning weeping hysterically in bed, I had to deal with the utter shit-show the band left me at the hotel. I ran around trying to convince the hotel not to sue us instead of crying my eyes red.

I soothed the hotel manager for an hour and gave him way more money than the budget could handle. Then, with my own money, I got ten-dollar Starbucks cards for every single member of the cleaning staff.

As soon as that was taken care of, I headed to the private airport nearby, to catch up with the band at the festival. Overton came too, which surprised me. I assumed he'd fly home now that our meeting was done. But then I realized, duh, of course he'd want to come. The band might hate festivals, but they were an excellent place to schmooze up-and-coming bands and poach talent.

I settled into the window seat next to Overton and gave him a tight little smile. If I wasn't so hung up on Mace and his stupid, but absolutely jacked, body, I could see being charmed by my boss's bullish ways.

He was a ridiculously charismatic minotaur. He flirted as easily as he breathed and when he stared at you, it was like you were the only person in the room. But I braced myself for a total ass-reaming for letting the band party out of control, figuring he'd be super pissed about the whole thing.

Instead, he smiled at me cheerfully. "Last night got pretty wild, huh?"

I kind of shrugged, "Yeah, I can't believe I missed the whole thing, I crashed out pretty hard early on and didn't get any news until Shawna busted into my room."

"Eh, they've been on a pretty short leash for a while, I'm surprised it took them so long to have a wild throw down."

I tried to keep the confusion off my face. "You guys expected them to trash a hotel?"

Overton chortled. "Don't get me wrong, we can't have them trashing all the hotels every night, but an over-the-top blow out every so often? It's pretty good for keeping them in the public eye as the "bad orcs of rock," you know?"

"But the loss of hotel rooms for the rest of the tour? I thought that was incredibly bad news."

"I got some PR flacks on it at the label, worst case the band has to bunk in the bus for a few days while you guys pull something together."

"Oh. Okay, I thought the tour might get canceled." My mind reeled, and everything I thought I knew was going up in smoke.

"Are you kidding? After the news of last night filtered out, their album is already up 10 slots on the big three streaming apps." He laughed at me. "I forget you're used to the boy-band life. We're beyond thrilled you managed to reel them in as long as you did but we don't expect you to be a miracle worker. AxeBender is, at the end of a day, one of the top Orc Rock bands and their fans expect them to be wild and free."

"So, you aren't going to fire me and Shawna for mishandling things?"

Overton's shoulders shook as he laughed. "You guys are a killer team, no way we want to mess with that."

Would he'd still think that if he realized I'd been banging Mace six ways to Sunday? And that we'd had a stupid fight, that possibly precipitated last night's antics?

"Not gonna lie, Jay, that's a relief. They'd been so chill, last night really took us by surprise."

Overton signaled the flight attendant for another drink. "Nah, don't sweat it. Although, keep this between us. The band may or may not have told you yet, but this festival? It was a real fucking bad scene last time they played. If you can, keep a tight eye on Mace. And if he starts acting funny, tell Frey immediately."

"Tell Frey?"

"Look, if they haven't felt comfortable sharing, I don't wanna break confidence, it's not my story to tell. But it is our business if Mace can't handle it. It's where all the shit went down with his ex."

"Ohhh." I fought to keep myself steady and professional. "I've heard a little about that, but very low key. Is there anything in particular I need to know?"

"What I can share is that you must keep them away from Orkestra. They are the main headliners and the label wants their next album, bad."

"Wouldn't making nice with Orkestra be smarter? Shawna is great at connecting with bands. Like, unnaturally charismatic."

"Look, you didn't hear it from me, but the ex, Aubrey? She tours with Orkestra now. Get it?"

"Oh, I see. Yeah." I could definitely put two and two together. "So, I'll loop Shawna in and we will make sure the bands never bump into each other."

"The festival organizers know all the hot gossip about everything and everyone, so they will make sure they aren't near each other, but there is a lot of free time, that's where you guys will need to be on point."

I winced to myself. Good thing I fought with Mace right before a potentially volatile working situation. Great. Just great. But I slapped a pleasant smile on my face. "No problem, boss. We will keep everyone in their respective corners."

Overton patted my hand and threw back his drink. "Honestly, AxeBender in general aren't especially confrontational. But again, between you and me, Orkestra loves having beef with everyone. Their publicists are firmly team 'any press is good press'."

With that, he leaned back into his seat and closed his eyes. He was snoring in the time it took me to blink. Definitely a skill worth having in our business.

My brain was churning too hard for me to settle in for a nap, so I stared out the window and thought. Even if hooking up with Mace had been amazing, clearly it was a terrible idea. Look at where it had gotten us. I hated that I put him in a vulnerable position right before a potentially calamitous meeting at the festival.

I should have kept my lust to myself. Stupid hot sexy orcs with their abs and their faces and hands. *God, their hands.*

When we landed, I got a text from Shawna. "Hey girl. Good news, bad news. Good news: I handled the hotel situation for the rest of the tour. Bad news? Our suite's going to be a little smaller than last time. The bigger ones are all booked..."

I was so relieved and poked Overton. "Dude, Shawna really is a rock star in her own right. She got the hotel situation taken care of."

"I knew you guys could handle it."

Much as I wanted this tour to be over, having it canceled for lack of hotel space would be awful for everyone else. I'd spent all day imagining losing my job over it, practically hearing the snide jabs my sister would make at Thanksgiving. I'd had to keep reminding myself that Overton said the label had faith in us. The label wasn't my terrible family. They weren't hoping to see me stumble.

Now I couldn't stop wondering how Shawna had managed to pull it off. I'd honestly believed that the best we could hope for was no one at the fleabag no-tell-motel noticing us when we snuck in. In the time I'd been in the air and out of contact, the news of the latest trashed room had already spread far and wide. A lot of party goers posted a lot of pictures on a lot of different social media sites.

A lot.

Shawna was a freaking miracle worker.

Chapter Thirty-Five

ALEXIS

Overton headed to the hotel and I headed off to the festival. When I arrived, everything was enjoyable chaos. Most people don't realize how much work goes into a festival beforehand. Bands don't show up, walk on, play and go home. Stages get set up and all the different areas are contained and the med tent and the backstage tents and all of it.

Thank god I had so much to do, it kept my mind off my aching, broken heart. I ran around for a few hours, making sure my team—crew and band alike—were taken care of. Luckily, Orkestra wasn't due to arrive until later in the day, so I could easily keep the bands apart.

It was well into late afternoon when I finally collapsed into a chair at craft services. I'd been thinking I should have a salad or something, but somehow found a burger, fries, and milkshake in front of me.

I'd only been eating for a few minutes when a tall, slim woman I didn't recognize put her tray down across from me. The pointiness of her ears told me she was part elf, but her smile was all human.

"Do you mind if I join you?" she asked in a low, musical voice. I shook my head, and she sat. "You're the new manager for AxeBender, right?"

I nodded. "Alexis," I said. It was all I could manage through my full mouth. Luckily I was able to cast a very brief illusion so she didn't see the food I was still chewing.

She smiled. "I'm Irvania. I manage Polar Frost."

I definitely knew who Polar Frost was, a band of werebears that had been around forever. The kind of band that was always on top-twenty lists, but never at number one. I'd heard they were a great band to tour with, laid back and happy. They might party as hard as the next rock star, but at least they didn't trash hotel rooms.

Among the road crews, their manager was way more famous than they were. Something of a legend, in fact. Known for making everything run perfectly and leaving every venue better than she found it, all while balancing a drink in one hand and a panicked venue owner in the other.

Suddenly nervous, I finally managed to swallow, and stuck out my hand. "It's very nice to meet you," I said. "Everyone says you're the best."

She raised an eyebrow. "The best? Not that it's not true," she said archly, "but who's been kissing and telling?"

My eyes widened, and she laughed. "Sorry," she said. "I get uncomfortable with compliments and so I deflect with dirty jokes. But thank you, it's nice to hear that one's work is appreciated." She peered at me. "Goodness, child, are you blushing?"

I turned quickly to my french fries. "No." I somehow turned even redder. As if this week couldn't get any worse, I was going to embarrass the shit out of myself in front of the freaking legendary Irvania.

She laughed again, and turned the conversation to how the festival set-up was going. In the next half hour, I learned more than I would have dreamed possible about working with venue managers, roadies, crews and bands, keeping everyone happy, making everything run together like it was built that way.

She didn't lecture or seem to intend to teach, just described how she'd spent her day and gave me gentle suggestions for the snags I'd hit in my own arrangements.

"You were a late add to the lineup, weren't you?" she asked as we were finishing our food. "Put in after SinBop dropped out?"

"That's right," I said. "One of our label execs flew out last night. I didn't hear what happened with SinBop, though. Only that they were being very flakey and suddenly we got their spot. Do you know what's up?"

"Oh everyone knows." She leaned forward and lowered her voice a bit, which didn't seem necessary if everyone knew. "The guitarist, Nancy Do, eloped with Bob, the guy in charge of their merch. Apparently she's pregnant, and I can't imagine how they would know that it's his, but I guess they're pretty excited to be parents."

I tried to wrap my head around this. "She and the merch guy?" I finally managed. "Did people know they were together? It seems like that could get ugly, a band member sleeping with a crew person."

Fuck, no wonder they got dropped if a band member and a crew member were screwing around. My mouth dried out as I thought about how bad it would have been to be caught fucking Mace, and how my lust for him could have ruined everything for the whole band.

Chapter Thirty-Six

ALEXIS

Irvania stared at me like I'd grown a second head. "You're kidding, right?" she asked, then her face cleared. "You used to manage a tween band, didn't you?"

I nodded and she laughed.

"This is a different world, honey. This is rock-and-roll on tour. Everybody is sleeping with everybody." She turned to the crowd around us, and started pointing out people she'd slept with. There were a lot of them. Some of them awfully famous. Elves were known for their appetites, but even so, this was impressive.

Then she went on to who else was sleeping with who, who had been secretly mated for years, who had recently broken up. My mind reeled a bit.

"I won't even get into the shapeshifters," she added, leaning in a little. "Let's say a lot of them have learned to control which parts of them shift." My face burned.

"But doesn't the label know about this?" I asked. "Don't they get upset? It seems awfully unprofessional."

She snorted. "'Unprofessional' means different things in different professions. Around here, 'unprofessional' is taking so many shrooms you puke on stage and can't continue the show. Having sex behind the scenes doesn't even register."

She grinned as she answered the question about the label's feelings about it all. "The higher-ups at the label pretend not to know about it. The lower level execs, they got into the business because they love music and didn't want a boring life. They're as bad as everybody else. Or as good, depending how you look at it."

I shook my head. "The ones I've met aren't like that."

"You sure? You say an exec flew out a couple times during the tour, including last night, right? To tell you the tour was changed a little? Something that could have been a call or an email? Who was it?"

I gulped. "Jay Overton."

She snorted again. "Jay Overton? Oh, he's a total babe. How was that cute drummer of yours this morning? Did it seem like she was in a real, real good mood?"

"I didn't see her," I said, shocked at the insinuation. "But you can't be saying–"

"Overton and Frey have been hooking up for *ages*. They think it's a secret, which is hilarious. I think they're scared that if they tell anyone they'll have to admit it's more than sex. I know for a fact he hasn't looked at anyone else in forever. And sure, her post-show orgies are absolutely legendary, but ever notice how she's always watching—but not doing anything else? They're mad for each other and don't want to admit it."

I shook my head. I mean, I knew about the orgies, but Frey didn't trash hotel rooms, so I stayed out of her business. I had no idea what she got up to in her spare time.

"Are you sure?" Even as I said it I remembered what an odd hurry he'd been in the night before. And how distracted he was, how he didn't seem to care that Mace and I were coming out of a storage closet. Care or even really notice. *Oh god.*

I leaned forward and said as casually as I possibly could, "But surely, not all relationships would be okay, right? I mean if, say, a tour manager and a member of the band were hooking up. Not that that would happen. But if it did, people would think the manager was indecorous, right?"

Her eyebrow arched again and she cocked her head with a little grin on her face, but if she guessed the question wasn't hypothetical, she pretended not to. "It happens all the time. Of course, it could be a problem, if there was a big age difference, and an experienced manager was convincing someone in a new band that it was necessary for their career—" She wrinkled her nose in distaste. "That would get nipped in the bud, fast. People keep an eye out for that sort of thing. It's also why it's always good to have shifters on the roadie crew. They can sniff it out.

"But if they're the same age? Established? Equals?" She took a long swig of her drink, which I suspected was more than just soda, and shrugged. "Why on earth not? If nothing else, it passes the time. And lord knows, there is a lot of time to kill on tour."

"So why don't we ever hear about it?" I asked. "I mean, why don't fans hear about it?"

"Because generally speaking, fans don't hear about relationships unless someone famous is dating someone else famous. It kills the dream to know a rock star is monogamous. So until there's marriage and babies, it's an open secret." She smiled. "It's okay, sweetie. You're adorable and if someone has noticed, and you like them noticing, go for it."

An hour later, I was sitting behind a tent, trying for the hundredth time to compose a text to Mace. I was an idiot, a complete and total idiot. Despite the fact that I was absolutely nuts about him, I'd put us both through agony. What could I say that would make him forgive me?

No wonder he'd been so confused. I was freaking out about my boss catching me getting off with the lead singer at the very moment my boss was getting off with the drummer.

I was still typing and erasing, typing and erasing, when my phone rang. It was Shawna.

"Please tell me you aren't calling with bad news about the hotels." Even though she'd said it was all taken care of, I was nervous. The last thing I wanted, now, was to be trapped on a bus with the whole band and near-zero privacy to give a lot of forgive-me blowjobs.

"The hotels are good." Shawna said chipper as always. "I told you, I figured it out."

"You are amazing," I breathed in relief. "How did you do it?"

"Oh, it wasn't too complicated," she said, in a voice that indicated that maybe she wasn't being entirely honest. "We now have an exclusive deal with the Corridon hotel chain for as long as we need them. They're very happy to be the official hotel of the AxeBender band."

"Why?" I asked, without thinking. "I mean, good. Great! You are a wonder."

Shawna's smile could be heard in her voice. "I do my best."

"How's– How's the band doing?" I asked. "They recovering?"

"Frey looks like she had a weekend at a spa," Shawna reported. "And Torch seems shaky but okay. He apologized, very, very sweetly. Jax and Clash slept for a while, but now they're up. Mace has been asleep for most of the ride."

I wanted to ask more about him, but didn't quite dare. "So they're in good spirits, overall?"

"I wouldn't say that. They've been back there talking for the past hour or so, all but Mace, and they seem upset. I think they're worried about whether they fucked up with the hotel. I'm not telling them yet that I worked it out. Let them suffer. Anyway, we'll be there in a couple of hours. You can head to the hotel if you want. I'll text you the address."

Suddenly desperate for a bath and a nap, I hopped in a Lyft and directed the driver to the hotel. Shawna's claim that our suite wouldn't be huge turned out to be incorrect—it was massive and gorgeous. If I had anything to do with it, Shawna was getting a gigantic raise. The label owed her big time.

Figuring my text to Mace could wait a while since he was asleep anyway, I took a long, long bath in the huge tub. I drafted and redrafted the text in my head, until it was *perfect*. Finally, I leaned back and let my body relax, releasing all my pent-up anxiety, drifting in and out of sleep as I imagined how much fun it would be to make up.

Assuming he forgave me.

Chapter Thirty-Seven

MACE

By the time the bus pulled up to the hotel, I had a plan. I'd head to my room, stay there until the show, and head straight back after. No lingering in public and social areas, definitely no parties. There was no reason I had to bump into Aubrey as long as I was careful.

In a few days we'd be moving on, and maybe I could start to try to figure things out with Alexis. Not a problem. I had a plan. First avoid my ex, and then getting Alexis to forgive me was top priority.

The plan was ruined ten seconds after I walked into the hotel lobby, when a familiar soprano voice squealed "Macey!" and a warm, soft, red-headed girl hurtled into my arms.

"Aubrey!" I said through gritted teeth, holding her away from me, even though her scent was filling my brain and my initial instinct was to pull her close. But that was muscle memory and as I stood there, I realized that under her stifling floral perfume was a distinct impression of rot and decay.

"Oh Macey, it's so good to see you!" Aubrey said, staring up into my face with her big green eyes. For a moment, I remembered our good times and how beautiful she was. But then I remembered walking in on her with Lewd and how she shrugged when I asked how she could do that to me.

Suddenly a large green hand clamped on my shoulder. "Mace, need anything?" Torch asked gruffly. I turned to see my whole band standing around me, glaring at my ex-girlfriend.

"No, it's okay," I said, wanting them to leave and hoping they wouldn't.

"Macey and I are going to catch up for a minute," Aubrey said in the baby voice she used when she was trying to be cute. I used to think it was cute, too, but now it was oddly grating. "You can go," she added, steel entering her tone as she glared back at them.

"No thanks," Jax said coldly.

"We like being with Mace too," Clash said. He had his usual jovial smile on his face, but his eyes were like glittering flint.

Frey growled softly.

People were starting to stare. Phones were going to come out soon. "It's okay, you guys, really," I said. "I'm going to talk to Aubrey for a minute. It's fine."

None of them seemed to think it was fine at all, but they'd also noticed the onlookers and moved away. Clash and Jax started showing off a bit, strutting around the lobby, pulling attention from me. I turned back to Aubrey.

"How're you doing?" I asked, trying to sound as cool as possible even though my heart was hammering. It was the first time I'd seen her since that last big fight.

"I'm doing okay." She smiled coyly and played with her hair. "Missing you."

I gulped. I felt almost nothing for her, but she was definitely trying to push my buttons. "Oh yeah?"

"Yeah," she said with a giggle. "Maybe we could go somewhere, hang out for a while?"

My brain short-circuited when she licked her lips. For a moment I forgot what she'd done to me, how it had broken me. Then my phone binged. I pulled it out and looked down, the words pulling me out of my daze.

"Mace—I'm an idiot. Can we talk? Rm 701."

And just like that, the memories of the good times I had with Aubrey dissipated. Whatever we'd had didn't hold a candle to how Alexis made me feel. "Maybe later, babe," I said. "Gotta run. Good to see ya!"

I all but ran for the elevators, not even bothering to glance over my shoulder to see the look on her face.

I broke several land speed records to get to room 701 and almost knocked the door down, but Alexis opened it before I could. I took her in my arms and pressed my lips to hers, and something that never happened with Aubrey flooded my body. Pure, unabashed joy. I'd felt happy with Aubrey, but never comfortable, or myself. It was like I had to be someone else to have her.

Whatever old residual feelings I had for Aubrey were absolutely obliterated by the mere touch of Alexis' hands.

"Mace, I'm so sorry—" I cut her off before she could finish her sentence.

"You don't have to apologize," I said. "You have nothing to apologize for." I remembered something they said that often at the recovery ranch.. "It doesn't matter if I don't understand why something upsets you," I told her. "What matters is that it does upset you. I promise, I'll never ignore you like that again. In fact—"

I picked her up and carried her through the suite to her bed, "I'm going to prove exactly how attentive I can be, right now." I laid her down and placed my hands on her ankles, spreading her legs apart. I paused and enjoyed the view of her sweet little pussy under her dress.

I growled in delight. "I love that you still skipped panties, in spite of our fight. Were you thinking about me when you got dressed?"

I didn't wait for an answer. I stroked my hands up her legs, pushing up the bottom of her dress as I went. I nibbled my way up her thighs, but I was too eager to taste her to linger, to tease. I flattened my tongue and swept from the bottom of the seam of her sex and circled her clit. She buried her hands in my hair and her thighs clasped my face.

I was in heaven.

I fucked her with my tongue as she arched off the bed, screaming my name. I needed to feel her come on my face, I needed to stake my claim on her. Her arousal soaked my face as I moved my lips to her clit. I slid two fingers where my tongue had been, plunging deep into her, crooking my fingers to catch that sweet bundle of nerves as I sucked on her clit.

She exploded all over my face, but I was relentless. I didn't let her catch her breath as I kept plundering her with my tongue and hands until another round of contractions throbbed around my fingers.

She went limp as I pulled myself to her, pressing my face against hers, capturing her mouth with mine as she trembled in my arms.

Chapter Thirty-Eight

ALEXIS

I could taste my arousal on his lips, the taste of his mouth mixing with the sweetness of my honey. Mace had been in my room for maybe five minutes and I'd already come twice. From the way he was kissing me, I was pretty sure I wasn't going to be able to walk tomorrow.

I was totally okay with that outcome.

As I floated on the waves of pleasure, I realized that we were still completely dressed. Unacceptable. I needed to feel Mace's skin against mine. I pushed him gently until he rolled onto his back, then I straddled him. He looked up at me, his blue eyes blazing with heat, and I ground down on his length, reveling in the wildness I saw enter his eyes.

I was equally as wild for him, I needed every inch of him in me. I grabbed the front of his shirt and with a strength that startled me, I tore it right off.

"I'll fix that later."

"I don't give a fuck about that shirt, that was the hottest thing that's ever happened to me."

As I pulled my dress over my head, Mace reached down and unbuttoned his jeans. I rose up on my knees, giving him a chance to wiggle them down a little, before I settled back down on his cock. The skin-on-skin contact against my still-sensitive pussy almost made me come again. I used my body to rub against the ridges of his cock, letting each one rub at my clit.

Mace's hands fisted the duvet as I rode him, until I was close to coming again, but this time I needed to come around his cock. I rose up until I nearly lost him, then reached between us and pressed the blunt crown against my entrance. Slowly I lowered myself down his shaft. It was agonizing to take him so slowly, but it was everything to see the look on his face, to see his body gleaming with a faint sheen of sweat. I stretched around each ridge until I bottomed out at the base and Mace started begging.

The thrill of the power I had over him made my skin hum and I leaned forward, resting my hands on his chest. "Do you want me, Mace?" I felt sultry and sexy as I raised my body away from him.

"Fuck, yes, Alexis. I want you. I need you. You're everything." I dropped back down on him, we both screamed and I used my leverage to ride him like my life depended on it. I was determined to make him completely lose control. Except then his hands wrapped around my hips and we were thrusting together and white lights shattered behind my eyes. I exploded around him as I felt his cock thicken and then pulse, filling me with his seed. I collapsed forward on his chest, his cock still hard in me.

This time he flipped me over and despite the tangle of his jeans, he kept thrusting into me. All I could do was hold on as he filled me over and over again, and a fresh orgasm built up.

His gaze caught mine and I was pinned down, screaming his name again.

"Yes, baby, yes. I need you to come again for me. I need to feel that pussy wrapped around my cock."

He picked up his pace until I couldn't hold back and I came again, the pulsing of my core pushing him over the edge. He exploded in me and I felt wave after wave of his come filling me yet again. We collapsed onto the bed, panting.

Mace said, "I'm so not done with you, but I am going to take my pants off first."

I giggled and realized I was still wearing my shoes and my bra. I sat up, unhooked my bra and tossed it next to the bed, my shoes following shortly after. Mace stood at the foot of the bed, getting his boots and jeans off before turning back to me. His cock jutted out in front of him. His eyes glinted as he stared at me.

"I guess you weren't kidding when you said you weren't done with me." I should have been utterly spent, too exhausted to go on, but seeing him? I wanted to feel him between my legs again.

"I need to get a Gatorade." He strode across the room to the minifridge, drank the Gatorade in one gulp, and turned back to me. A feral, wild grin crossed his face as he stalked back to the bed. He grabbed my ankle and pulled me to the edge of the bed. His movements were strong and sure as he flipped me to my stomach then pulled me up to my knees. "Are you ready?"

"Fuck, yes, Mace. I'm so ready for you."

He rubbed his hand against my opening until I was dripping with need, then pressed against me. As he slammed into me, each ridge rubbed me the right way and my fingers curled into the covers. One of his hands fisted into my hair, pulling my head back as he thrust into me. His other hand, wet with my arousal, pressed against the rosebud of my ass.

I gasped as his thumb pressed past the ring of resistance. I'd never been touched there before and it was a little shocking. I wasn't sure if I should protest, but it felt so good when it stretched and filled me. He rode me hard, filling me with his cock and his finger as wave after wave broke over me. As I contracted around his cock, he thrust faster, until he filled me with his seed once more.

Chapter Thirty-Nine

MACE

I lay back on the bed next to her, exhausted. "I don't have a show today, do I?" I panted.

"Nope," she said, tracing my chest lightly with her fingers. "Not till tomorrow night."

"Thank god," I said. "I've got no energy left."

"Well, I have kind of a problem," Alexis told me, her voice pouty and playful.

"What's that?"

"I know you're tired," she said, slowly trailing her fingers down my stomach. "But I can't keep myself away from this cock."

She gripped my shaft lightly but firmly, her fingers barely reaching halfway around it. It was as hard as it had been before we'd started. A little harder maybe, if that was possible.

"So I was thinking," she continued, "What if you lie there, I climb on top of you, ride you like a maniac, and we'll see how many times I come before you fill me with more of your hot come?"

I half-groaned, half-laughed, and pulled her on top of me. "Do your worst," I growled, "but maybe let's drink some more Gatorade first, okay?"

When I woke up the next morning I was as erect as ever, and I realized I was going to have to fuck Alexis yet again. Luckily she was as eager as she had been the night before, and I once again sprayed come all over her.

"Fuck me, Mace. How can you keep going?"

"The joy of being an orc."

Alexis snorted at me and pushed me off the bed after she checked the time. "Damn, as much as I want to spend all day in bed, I need to hit the shower."

"I'll go find my room, get showered and changed, and meet you at the buffet for breakfast?"

"Good plan. Now go before I decide I need another orgasm."

At some point the night before we'd ordered room service. I could barely remember it, but the remains of our dinner were still on the mahogany desk across from Alexis' bed. We must have eaten but after our night, I was absolutely ravenous.

I hadn't even gotten my room key yet, so I went down to the desk and then back up to the seventh floor. My room was huge, not as nice as Alexis' suite but a lot nicer than what we were used to.

In fact, it reminded me of the rooms we used to get to stay in—before we got a reputation for trashing rooms. I wondered how Shawna had pulled that off. I was pretty sure she wasn't a witch, too, but she must have some sort of magic.

As I walked down the hall to the elevators, Aubrey suddenly stepped out in front of me. I had completely forgotten she was around. "Macey!" she squealed, "where did you go last night? I looked everywhere for you!"

"Why?" I asked bluntly. "Why weren't you with Poo—I mean, Lewd?"

Her big eyes filled with tears. "He broke up with me, Macey," she said in a tragic whisper. "He was horribly cruel, and made up all sorts of reasons, but the truth is—" She moved in closer than I liked. I backed up till I hit the door of the elevator behind me. "I think he knew that deep down, I was still in love with you." She looked up at me with her huge green eyes, and the only emotion that burbled out of me was scorn. So that was it. She'd been dumped by the bigger star and now she was running back to me.

"Look, Aubrey," I said firmly. "It's *never* going to happen again with us. We're over. For good. You made your choice, and I've moved on."

ALEXIS

After slipping into my clothes, I finally picked up my phone and saw the headlines. My heart sank into the floor when the pictures loaded. It was the lobby of our current hotel, Aubrey looking up with Mace with bright eyes and the look in his eyes and tilt of his head.

It was how he had looked when he gazed at me. At least, I thought that's how he looked. I shook my head, I'd already made one set of assumptions. I'd pop down to his room and we could talk. It clearly wasn't an old picture, but every picture tells a thousand lies.

I headed down the hallway. And there they were. *Together*.

MACE

"Don't say that, Macey," Aubrey purred. "What we have will never go away."

I didn't expect what happened next, or I would have stopped it. A man stepped out of the stairwell and distracted me. Her ridiculous high heels made her almost as tall as me and suddenly, out of nowhere as far as I was concerned, she leaned in and kissed me. There was a sudden flash of lights out of the corner of my eye from the man as he captured Aubrey planting one on me.

And at that exact goddamn moment, Alexis came around the corner.

I'd already started pushing Aubrey off even before I saw Alexis, but as soon as our eyes met I knew—Alexis thought I was kissing Aubrey on purpose.

Alexis turned and ran back down the hall. Aubrey staggered back, calling my name and grasping at me as I chased after the one woman I cared about, the one woman I actually wanted to be with.

I turned back and snapped at Aubrey. "Get the fuck away from me." I shook her hands off me.

Her face twisted into an angry grimace. "I'll make you regret this, Mace." She grabbed the man who'd popped out and taken the pictures, and shoved him into the now-open elevator. "You'll always be second best, Mace. Never a first choice."

It should have hurt, but mostly I felt relieved that Aubrey was gone and I could focus on finding Alexis. But I couldn't find her. I mean, I was pretty sure she'd gone to her suite, but I couldn't find the door marked 701. I know that makes no sense. But there was 700, then 702, 703—

After roaming up and down the hall a few times, I finally realized she must have done something to make it so I couldn't find her. I pulled out my phone, but her number was no longer in my contacts, and all our texts had disappeared.

I went back to my room and howled with rage. I couldn't control my body and I paced and punched the air while I screamed out my frenzy. My arm swept the bar top and the sound of shattering glass was balm to my soul.

Chapter Forty

ALEXIS

Misdirection spells were usually beyond me, but this time it was easy. All I had to do was think about it and I became invisible to those around me. I paced up and down the living room of my gigantic suite, secure in the knowledge that even if Shawna walked out of her bedroom right now, her eyes would slide right past me.

She didn't walk out, though. Luck was on my side and there was nobody to watch me disintegrate.

I shook my head, trying to clear it. I recognized that girl immediately. I knew who she was. *Aubrey*. Less than an hour after spending the night with me, Mace had "bumped" into Aubrey in the hall and had, apparently, fallen face first onto her lips.

My face burned. I was angry, but even more than that I was totally humiliated. Why had I trusted him? Why had I believed the lead singer of an orc rock band actually cared about me? I'd let my guard down with Mace, let him in, and now my heart was breaking into a million little pieces.

Much as I fought it, another image was rising in my mind, of Christopher and Jeanie. Christopher, my college boyfriend, and Jeannie, my college roommate and best friend. Former best friend. After three years of what I thought was perfect happiness, I'd discovered the two of them together.

And not only were they fooling around behind my back, a lot of our college "friends" knew about it, even helped them fool me. It was beyond humiliating, and I'd spent years trying to forget, trying to keep myself safe. It was why I'd barely dated in so long, why my last long-term "relationship" was with someone I only knew online—until I met "him" and he turned out to be an old lady with a lot of parrots.

With Mace, I'd finally let myself go—and now I was paying the price. The sharp, stabbing pain in my chest was just my love shattering my soul.

"I have to get out of here," I thought to myself. I couldn't stay. I couldn't face Mace, couldn't stand there while he explained that we were over, couldn't watch him with his arm around Aubrey. What if—*oh god*—what if he wanted to bring her on the tour bus?

I ran into my room and started throwing things into my bag haphazardly. In a few minutes I was headed for the door—but then I remembered Shawna. I couldn't disappear. That wasn't fair to her, I couldn't drag her down in my fuck-up. I grabbed paper and a pen off the table and began writing.

> *I'm sorry, Shawna. This gig isn't for me. I'm such an idiot, and Mace is back with Aubrey.*

I stopped, wondering why I'd written that part and whether I should erase it, but didn't bother.

> *I just can't. I'm taking off. You can manage them for the rest of the tour. You'll do great.*

I knew that wasn't nearly enough, but the misdirection spell started to slip. I wasn't ready to face anyone, I couldn't. I grabbed my bag and headed for the door. I went down the back stairs and out the lobby, taking off the spell as I arrived at the taxi stand.

It would mean people could text or call me again, but that was okay, I'd turn off my phone. I told the taxi driver to take me to the bus station and held my breath the whole way there.

I bought the cheapest ticket and got onto a bus headed to a town a few hours away. I turned off my phone, vowing not to turn it on again for at least a few days. It wasn't really fair to Shawna but I couldn't endure the same mortification that I'd felt back in college.

I couldn't stand to face the whole band and know they knew about my humiliation. God, the whole festival would know.

When the bus stopped, I wandered the depot for a while, aimlessly, until I finally realized how exhausted I was. I grabbed a taxi, slumped in the back seat, and asked the driver to take me to the nearest hotel. His eyes met mine in the rearview mirror.

"Lady," he said, "I wouldn't advise a rat to stay at the nearest hotel."

I racked my brain and remembered the name of the hotel I'd left. "Okay, is there a Corridon around here?"

"Sure," the driver said, putting the car in gear and slowly pulling into traffic. "Corridon hotels are everywhere."

The lobby of the hotel was pretty much exactly like the one I'd stayed at the night before, but my room was nowhere near as nice. I had to budget carefully, now that I was out of a job—or would be, as soon as I got it together enough to call Overton and quit.

But I didn't care what the room was like. I didn't care about anything. I sank down onto the bed and finally allowed myself to cry and cry and cry.

Chapter Forty-One

MACE

I lay on my bed, feeling like I wanted to die. After half an hour of staring at the ceiling with no idea what to do, I checked my phone for the thousandth time and to my astonishment found that Alexis' phone number was back in my contacts.

Whatever spell she'd cast was gone.

Hoping this meant she was ready to talk, I called her immediately. Straight to voicemail. So I texted her.

Alexis, please, it wasn't what it looked like.

I frowned. That sounded ridiculous. I deleted it and tried again.

> *Alexis, I swear, she kissed me before I knew what was happening. I hadn't even had a chance to push her off me when you came around that corner.*

That was a little better. I couldn't think of anything else. I sent the text. The word "delivered" appeared, and I stared at the screen for ages, waiting for it to change to "read." But that didn't happen.

I finally threw the phone down and paced up and down the room. I should call Shawna. Or Frey. Frey might know what to do. But I couldn't bring myself to face any of them.

Of course it wasn't long before they came to me. Roughly half an hour after I sent the text to Alexis, there was pounding on the door. I opened it, hoping that maybe, somehow, it might be her.

It was not.

My whole band filed into my room, followed closely by Shawna. They stood in a half-circle around me, glaring.

"What, what now?" I asked, sitting on my bed and putting my head in my hands.

"Are you," Frey's voice asked, her voice strangled and sounding like her jaw was clenched tight, "back together with Aubrey?"

"What?!" My head snapped up and I stared at them. "No, no of course not! Why would you think that?"

"Because that's what Alexis says in this note," Shawna spat, waving a piece of hotel stationary at me. "The note she left in our room before she quit."

"And that's what the tabloids are all screaming. A picture of you and fucking Aubrey who almost destroyed the band *kissing!*" Mild mannered Torch was screaming at me.

But all I could focus on was Shawna's statement. "Quit?" I stared at her blankly. "What do you mean, quit??"

"What do you think I mean?" Her eyes flashed red and she looked furious. I remembered what I'd thought the first time I met her, that there was something about her that made me never want to fight her.

I'm pretty sure I was about to find out why I'd felt that way. And my bandmates would only help hide my body.

Shawna advanced on me, her voice clipped and brusque. "Alexis left a note telling me that she was leaving the tour, that she was upset because she'd seen you making out with Aubrey."

"How the hell could you?" Torch glared at me. "I mean it's bad enough that you would get back together with Aubrey, but how could you do that to Alexis?"

The rest of my bandmates grumbled in angry agreement while I stared at them.

"You know about me and Alexis?" I asked stupidly.

"Of course we know," Jax snapped. "Literally everyone knows. It's the most obvious thing in the world."

"To be honest it was kind of adorable," Clash added. "The two of you, constantly needing to leave at the same time, then running off in opposite directions." His face darkened. "Well, adorable until you cheated on her."

"I did not cheat on her!" I exploded. "Aubrey caught me in the hall and I was telling her it was absolutely, one hundred percent over between us, when she kissed me out of nowhere. And before I could even react, Alexis came around the corner." I looked from face to face, inwardly begging them to believe me. "I felt nothing in that kiss. The only one I want to kiss is Alexis."

They stared at me. "For real?" Frey finally asked. "Hogtie promise?"

"Hogtie promise!!" I practically yelled it, and my band relaxed.

"What the hell does 'hogtie promise' mean?" Shawna asked, still glaring and clearly still ready to dismember me.

"It's from when we were kids," Torch told her. "It means if we're lying, the others can hogtie us and leave us outside overnight."

"But really," Jax added, "it just means, like, really honestly for real."

Clash nodded. "None of us would ever, *ever* lie about a hogtie promise. He's telling the truth."

Shawna was still unsure. She looked at Torch. "You're absolutely certain? He's not lying?"

Torch nodded. "Absolutely certain."

Shawna sighed, some of the despair leaving her face, but not all of it.

"Well that's good. The problem is how to get Alexis to believe you."

"Maybe if you all come with me when I go talk to her?" I asked. "You could back me up? Say you believe me, and that it's the kind of thing Aubrey would do?" It sounded pathetic, even to me. I shouldn't need back-up when talking to my girl.

Shawna scowled again. "That might work, if we had any idea where she was or how to reach her. But we do not."

"Feather mitts," I said, using an old orc swear that was reserved for the worst situations. Jax actually gasped. "I can't lose her. She's the most wonderful woman I've ever met."

No one spoke. I didn't blame them for not knowing what to say.

"Maybe if I text her again," I said. "Tell her I'm sorry, tell her I love her—"

This time all of them gasped. "Wait, you love her?" Torch asked. "Seriously?"

I stared at the floor and nodded. I loved her. I had loved her from the first moment our eyes met, really, in that terrible little green room, when I accidentally insulted her because I was so taken aback by how damned sexy she was. Every moment I'd known her, I'd loved her more.

"Okay," Frey said suddenly, loudly. "We're going to fix this. Shawna, go find out where Alexis is. You'll figure it out, you know everyone she knows."

Shawna nodded. "And what do I do when I find her?"

"You bring her back. And then, well, I don't know exactly. Still figuring it out. I'll text you."

Shawna nodded and pulled her phone from her pocket as she headed for the door. The sense of purpose shone off her like gold dust, and I believed she would find a way. She'd worked a miracle with the hotels, she had to be able to find Alexis. And from the way her fingers flew across the keyboard on her phone, I think she was gonna make it happen.

"Now," Frey said once Shawna left. "I have a plan. Part of a plan. But Mace, it's going to involve doing something you swore you'd never do."

I racked my brain. "Drink frog spawn?"

Frey shook her head. "Worse," she told me. "Much worse."

Chapter Forty-Two

ALEXIS

I was still lying on the bed, when a knock echoed against the door. I had cried myself to sleep. The room was dark, and my first thought was that I'd been out for the whole day, but glancing at the clock I realized it was only about six at night. I glanced at the window and the fading light of the sky. I'd never drawn the curtains. I turned on the light and sat up.

I was hazy and confused about being woken, until another series of knocks came. Whoever was on the other side of the door was impatient. I considered ignoring it, but either it was someone with the hotel, in which case that would be rude, or somehow it was one of my friends, in which case ignoring it probably wouldn't do much good. I finally walked across the room and peered through the peephole.

Shawna stood there, looking anxious but determined. I was immediately flooded with a torrent of mixed feelings. Even though none of them should know where I was, my heart still plummeted that it wasn't Mace, risking everything to drag me back. It was good to see Shawna—I definitely needed someone to talk to, the way I was feeling—and also a little awful to see her because I didn't know what to say and knew that she wouldn't go away in a hurry.

She had seen the peep hole go dark. "Alexis!" she called, "I know you're in there!"

How? How did she know where I was? How had she found me? Surely she didn't have access to my credit cards? That would be weird. I considered, again, not answering. But I knew too well how obstinate my friend could be. Sighing and giving in to the inevitable, I opened the door.

Shawna threw her arms around me. "Oh Alexis!" she gasped. "I was so worried about you!"

"I'm fine. I left a note," I protested, but my voice cracked a little. I was definitely not fine and it felt good to be hugged.

Eventually, Shawna pulled away and led me to a chair. "Sit," she commanded. She pulled a bottle of water out of her purse and handed it to me. "Drink!"

I drank. How had she known I was thirsty? Then I realized that it was probably obvious I'd spent ages crying. I drank more. When the bottle was half empty, I paused long enough to ask the obvious question. "How did you find me?"

Shawna opened her mouth to answer, but before she could speak there was a timid knock on the hotel room door, which I realized she hadn't closed.

"Ms. Withern?" a voice called.

"Yes, in here," Shawna answered. "Come right in."

The door swung open all the way and a young man in a hotel uniform entered, pushing a trolley laden with food: a tray of buffalo wings and jalapeno poppers, a six-pack of my favorite soda, a pitcher of water, a large fruit plate, a hamburger and fries, and two simply enormous ice cream sundaes. Shawna smiled. "Thank you, Max." She slipped him a folded bill and his eyes widened.

"Thank you, Ms. Withern. Anything you need, Ms. Withern. I'll be right outside if you need anything."

"Thank you Max, but that's not necessary. Please close the door on your way out."

"Of course, Ms. Withern." I watched in astonishment as the young man backed out of the room, almost bowing.

"What the hell was that all about?"

Shawna flushed. "I was going to tell you about it, I really was. I couldn't figure out a good way yesterday, and when I woke up this morning you were already gone."

"Tell me what?" I wouldn't have thought anything could distract me from my broken heart, but this was coming close.

"Well, you know yesterday morning, you told me to find hotels for the band to stay at, because all the hotels were canceling our reservations after they trashed their room?"

"Yes, Shawna, obviously I remember that. It was yesterday. And then you performed a miracle and got us an exclusive deal with the Corridon Hotel Chain."

"Right. Okay, well—" I'd never seen her this reluctant to talk. She looked away and spoke fast. "All the hotels were saying no, *all of them*, including the Corridon, and I was getting so desperate because I really didn't want the tour to end early. That'd be awful, and I started to panic that the record label might even drop them. So I—" she trailed off again. "I did something."

Suddenly extremely concerned, I leaned forward and put my hand on her shoulder. "Oh god, what did you do?" Visions of Shawna blackmailing CEOs flashed through my mind.

"Nothing like that," she said quickly, and I wondered what she thought I was thinking. Because I didn't know what to think.

Shawna took a soda from the trolley, opened it, took a long gulp, and said so fast it sounded like one word. "I called my accountant and bought the Corridon Hotel. I bought the chain of hotels, I mean. I own them now. That's how I got them to let us stay with them. Because I'm the one who decides that now. It's also how I found you. On the off chance you'd get a room at a Corridon, I told them to ping me if you checked in anywhere. And it worked."

I absent-mindedly cursed myself for not using a fake name, but I was too bewildered to worry about it much. I stared at her with my mouth open for a while, and eventually gathered my wits enough to speak. "I'm sorry, what?"

She seemed to be blinking back tears. "There's something I never told you."

"Yeah," I agreed. "That's very clearly the case. The fact that you can afford to buy a chain of hotels is something you definitely forgot to mention." The look on her face made me feel bad. "Not," I added gently, "that it is any of my business. And I am incredibly grateful that you saved us from sleeping on the bus every night. I'm just a little surprised. And confused."

Chapter Forty-Three

ALEXIS

Shawna nodded. "Okay, well, here it is. My family is very wealthy. Like, very very, very wealthy. Wealthier than however wealthy you're thinking. And while most of the family money is my grandmother's, I also kind of got some of my own, a trust. I mean, not some. A lot. Enough to start my own hoar—" She stopped again. "My own life. I went to college, and everyone treated me differently, because I was so rich. So I switched schools and pretended to be regular. And when I graduated and got a job, I decided to live on my income from that, like a normal person. I started some charities, but have a lot left over."

I sat back. "Okay," I said, starting to recover. "Well, thank you for sharing that with me. I promise not to pry again if it makes you uncomfortable."

"No, it's okay," she smiled. "I don't mind you knowing." She pulled the trolley closer. "Now, what would you like to eat first? I was thinking sundaes, 'cause they could melt, but maybe first you should eat something more substantial."

She offered me the burger, but I shook my head. "Sundae, please!"

She handed me one and took the other, and for a moment we concentrated on the hot fudge and whipped cream that smothered vanilla and chocolate ice cream.

Eventually, Shawna spoke again. "Endless ice cream sundaes are a pretty good perk, don't you think? And it'll be pretty fun to always stay in fancy suites from now on, right?"

I started to automatically nod in agreement, then flinched. "I won't be staying in any suites, Shawna. I'm not going back."

"But you have to," she said, putting down the sundae to show how serious she was. "Listen, Alexis, I know what you saw. But I talked to Mace, and I believe him. He's not back with Aubrey, and he's not cheating on you. He wasn't kissing Aubrey on purpose. She was setting him up with the paparazzi. That's why there is all sorts of tabloid nonsense."

I snorted. "What, he was kissing her by accident?"

"Yeah, kind of. I mean, it wasn't an accident on her end, but she leaned in and kissed him while he was telling her she meant nothing to him. You came around the corner at literally that second. Lewd dumped her ass and she's trying to keep a high profile so she can leech on to some other schmuck."

I thought back to the moment that was seared into my mind's eye. It was true, I came around the corner at the very moment of their kiss. I saw her leaning in. It was possible what Shawna was saying was true. I wanted to believe it. For a moment, I was tempted, but then I shook my head. "I can't, Shawna, I just can't. I can't make a fool of myself like that. Never again."

Her eyes narrowed. "What do you mean, *never again*?"

I took a large bite of sundae, and she waited patiently until I swallowed. "I told you I had a serious boyfriend in college, right? Christopher?"

She nodded, eating her sundae but not taking her eyes off me.

"Well, I told you we broke up at the end of college, but I didn't tell you why." She started to interrupt, but I held up my hand. "Wait, yes, I did tell you why, I told you we wanted different things. But the truth is—"

This was hard. It was the first time I'd told anyone since shortly after it happened.

"What I wanted was him, and what he wanted was my roommate. And he got her, and had her, for a good long time before I found out. Months, apparently."

Shawna gasped. "That's horrible!"

"Yeah. And a lot of our friends knew. When I asked a couple of them why they'd never told me, they said they'd figured it wasn't really their business, and they didn't want to hurt me." My mouth twisted into a painful smile. "And they said that everyone felt really, really bad for me. Felt *sorry* for me." I shuddered, hard, and shoved another huge spoonful of sundae into my mouth. All those people I'd thought were my friends, pitying me and letting me think everything was fine.

"Alexis, that's horrible," Shawna said. "I mean, I want to kill them both for doing that to you! But this is a totally different situation."

I shook my head. "Not different. Not really. I'm not going through that kind of humiliation again, Shawna. Not for anything. You can't—You can't imagine what it's like."

Her eyes flashed. "I can, Alexis. I really really can. Trust me. But this is different. No one feels sorry for you, just angry at Mace. Torch and all the others think you're the best thing that ever happened to him, and say if he fucks it up, they'll never forgive him. Every single person who knows about it—which is only the seven of us—all think he's the one who should be embarrassed. Not you."

"What about Aubrey? She knows they kissed. And I mean, there is a picture of them kissing in every single fucking tabloid."

Shawna rolled her eyes. "From what Torch said, once they have a minute to think about it, literally no one is going to believe her that they are back together. She's famous for making stuff up. 'Wouldn't believe her if she said it was raining in a typhoon,' were his exact words. It's not going to be a problem."

I chewed my lip. "You really think—?" I asked.

She nodded and took my hand. "I saw how distraught he was. I'm absolutely positive."

I groaned and fell back on the bed, reeling in shock. "This is horrible," I started to cry again. I'd fucked everything up by assuming Mace was anything like Christopher.

"What's horrible? It's a good thing! Why are you so upset?"

"Because I freaked out at him the other night over it not being professional for us to be together, and now I've freaked out on him again. I didn't even give him a chance to explain. I panicked and left. He must hate me."

"He doesn't hate you!" Shawna protested. "He—he doesn't hate you at all."

"Oh Shawna," I wailed. "He's the most wonderful man in the world, and now I've ruined everything!"

Chapter Forty-Four

*A**LEXIS*

Shawna came and sat down next to me on the bed. "Alexis, you haven't. I really, really don't think you have."

I wanted to believe her, but I couldn't. "You don't know," I said, shaking my head. "I wouldn't even let him explain. I actually cast a spell so he wouldn't be able to find me! How could I do something like that?"

"Well, in fairness to yourself, you did see another girl kissing him. And not just *any* girl. *The* girl you knew he used to be, like, super-duper in love with. Anyone would have freaked out."

"But less than forty-eight hours after my last freak out?'

"Also less than forty-eight hours after he trashed a room and almost got their tour canceled," she reminded me. "Listen, Alexis, you haven't ruined anything. But you might, if you don't come back *now*. We have to go to the concert tonight. Show him you're still crazy about him. Show him you believe him. You'll be glad you did. Honest."

I shook my head. I was so confused and sad.

"All right," Shawna said, a little bit of impatience creeping into her voice. "Tell you what. You don't want to try to get back with him, fine. But listen. If you don't come back, now, to the festival, you're done at the record label. Shit, with the entire industry. You've got to know that."

"I can't keep managing AxeBender, Shawna. How could I handle seeing him every day?"

"Fine, maybe you couldn't. But you have to quit properly. Call them, give them some reason why it's not working out. Say you have to take a break to help your family, say you have appendicitis, say anything. You'll take a couple weeks off, and they'll assign you to some other tour. But you've got to do this professionally, Alexis. Otherwise, there's no way they'll keep you on. You have to call them from the festival. You've worked way too hard to give up everything over some dick."

She was right. I knew she was right. I sat up. I wanted Mace, needed him, but I wasn't going to sacrifice everything I'd worked for because my heart was feeling a little battered.

"Maybe," I said. I looked towards the windows again, but the dim light didn't tell me much. I groped in the bed covers for my phone. "What time is it?"

Shawna had her phone out first. "Six o'clock."

"Shawna! We'll never make it back in time!" I leapt to my feet. I'd been so foolish. Shawna wouldn't be here if she didn't think there was hope, a chance for Mace and me. My life would be endless regret if I didn't at least talk to Mace again, see him, tell him I was sorry and that it's just that I fucking loved him and it was making me crazy.

Holy shit, I loved him.

"Hmm?" Shawna was ignoring me, staring at her screen, apparently engrossed in reading a text she'd received.

I shook her shoulder. "Shawna! It's too late. It will take hours to get back to the festival."

She finally looked at me. Stared at me. Narrowed her eyes, and they seemed to glint red-gold. "No, it won't," she said. "There's something else I haven't told you. Let's go up to the roof."

"What? Did you buy a helicopter too?"

"Oh no," Shawna said with a smile. "This is way better than a helicopter."

Chapter Forty-Five

MACE

I love the process of writing songs. It's almost always done the same way: Jax, Clash, and Torch go into one room and start working on the music while Frey and I sit and sketch out the words. Torch goes back and forth between rooms, figuring out what kind of music will match our lyrics and letting us know what music is happening so we can mold lyrics to it.

Writing with Frey has never been anything but fun. Even when we fight, we enjoy it.

This time was a little different. For one thing, it was a lot harder for the others to write the music in a hotel room because they couldn't play around on their guitars the way they usually did. But it was better for Frey and me, because room service is awesome.

Of course, the lyrics were also different than usual. And they mostly came from me, with Frey working on rhymes and word order and stuff. But it was still fun, and it made me forget, for a moment, my sadness and desperation as I poured my heart and soul through my pen. I held Alexis's face, her smile, in my mind as I opened my veins and let the words out.

We were done in time to run through it a few times before we had to head for the stage. We always pump one another up on our way to a show, jumping around and shouting and doing high kicks and cartwheels and flips—going to orc school three days a week after regular school was a pain in the ass, but it means we all know how to do awesome acrobatics, even though there's not a chance any of us will ever go to war. Between writing all day and then horsing around with my best friends, I was feeling hopeful.

The good feeling started to die while we were sitting backstage, waiting to go on. The band before us, an Emo-Orc band called 'Green Blood Tears' was taking forever to end their set, and so we were just hanging around. Torch reminded me to signal him when I saw Alexis or Shawna in the crowd, and he'd start the new song. I knew no one wanted to do it unless it was going to work, and it couldn't work if she wasn't there.

Immediately the fear that Alexis wouldn't believe Shawna came crashing down and all hope drained out of me. "What are the chances she'll even show up?" I asked. "And if they are there, how the hell will I spot them?"

Frey looked at her phone for the millionth time and frowned. I knew that meant there were no texts. "Dude, settle your hash. Shawna seemed pretty certain that once she found Alexis, she could convince her to come back. And in the last text, she said, 'trust me, if I'm back, you'll all know it.'. And Shawna won't be here unless Alexis is with her."

I nodded and tried to concentrate on the sound of the crowd outside. They sounded like a good audience, at least. That always helped.

As I paced, Frey suddenly started growling. And like a bad penny, Aubrey rolled up to me.

She twirled her hair around her finger and batted her eyelashes, but her eyes were ice cold. How had I ever imagined she was warm and caring? I was an idiot she'd completely snowed over.

"What on earth do you want, Aubrey."

She pouted. "Don't be mad at me."

"You set me up with the paparazzi. You got my face all over the tabloids." For once, instead of sadness or lust or whatever it was I had with Aubrey, there was only unadulterated rage at what a complete *asshole* she was.

She rolled her eyes. "You are welcome, by the way. It distracted from all your hotel wrecking stories." Had she always been so nasty?

"Yeah, by you using me for whatever the fuck it is you want."

She shrugged. "I'm not the one whose heart got broken. I was giving you another chance with me."

"Eww. Just eww. And if you and Lewd broke up, why are you even here? Why are you backstage?"

She tapped the pass around her neck. "I still have access. And as long as I stay out of Lewd's way until he's horny again, it's fine."

"Actually, it's not fine. You aren't okay, Aubrey. You are an unkind person and I don't actually have to put up with your bullshit."

"Uhm, don't talk to me like that. I thought I'd see if you wanted a quickie before your show. You used to love that." Her eyes gleamed and she stepped towards me.

Amazed that I'd once believed I loved her, I put my hand out and called, "Security! Please escort this groupie away from me."

"How dare you, I have a *pass*."

"And I'm a performer, and I can have you removed from the backstage area. Go back to whatever second-rate rock star you crawled out from under."

I turned my back on Aubrey as she shrieked at the security guards. Frey met my eyes and gave me a massive grin, while the boys clapped happily like the cheerful idiots they were.

"Whatever guys, and I'm sorry I saddled you with her for so freaking long."

They pushed me around and we all settled in to wait.

When it was finally time to go on, Alexis still hadn't returned. "This is all pointless," I muttered to Frey.

"No it's not," Frey looked up from her phone. "She'll be here by the last song."

"Well, if it works at all, she'll only need to be here for that song. How do you think our fans will react?"

"I think they'll love it."

"Seriously?"

"Okay, seriously I have no idea. But they might. And if they don't, we'll never do it again. It'll be a one-time special."

"Freya?"

"Yeah?"

"I don't really care if our fans like it."

Frey clapped me on the back. "I know, honey. I know."

We stepped out onto the stage and the familiar surge of adrenaline began to course through me. I'd always loved this moment, walking to the microphone, wrapping my hand around it, and looking out at the crowd. It was a burst of pure joy.

Torch struck the first chords of the song we always started with. I opened my mouth and a roar came out. I put my soul, all the pain of losing Alexis, and all my passion for her, into that roar.

But also the thrill of knowing that I was completely, utterly, entirely done with Aubrey, forever. The only woman who mattered to me was Alexis. I searched the crowd with my eyes, hoping I'd get the chance to tell her how I felt about her, about us.

I ached for her, to feel her in my arms, and I sang that ache to the crowd, even if the words were about mayhem and carousing. Surely she'd show up. She had to—she *needed* to know that I loved only her and never wanted to be with anyone but her, ever again.

Fifteen feet below us, the audience was reacting to my singing, clearly feeling the energy behind it even if they didn't know why the energy was there. The orcs in the crowd slammed together, the humans sometimes climbing on their backs and jumping off, to be caught by other orcs.

Shape-shifters—wolves and big cats and bears—shifted back and forth, human to creature to human again. It was entirely out of their control when they were dancing like this, and I loved having the power to let them safely lose themselves this way.

I grew more and more hopeful as the songs played. She would come. Surely she would come. She had to come. Again and again I searched the crowd. Frey had said that if Shawna was there, I'd see her. I didn't get how but maybe she'd made a necklace out of glowlights, or something.

And then, out in the night sky, I saw it.

Chapter Forty-Six

*A*LEXIS

I was a little nervous as I followed Shawna to the roof. I assumed that when she said she had something better than a helicopter, she must have a biplane or something, but the roof was entirely empty save a large, humming air conditioning unit.

"Okay," Shawna said, looking nervous but excited. "There's something else I have to tell you. But it's easier to show you than tell you. Please don't be scared. Stand back a bit."

Having someone tell you not to be scared can be pretty scary, especially when you're standing on a roof under a darkening sky. But I trusted Shawna, so I nodded and backed up.

Shawna stood very still for a moment. She closed her eyes, took a deep breath, and then she—grew. She grew and grew and grew. Her skin turned into scales of green and gold and red. Her face stretched long and her hair turned into a crown of spikes. Shawna's arms and legs flexed as claws sprouted from her fingertips, and gigantic wings unfurled from her shoulders.

It seemed to last an eternity but was over before I knew it. There, in front of me, was an absolutely massive, exquisitely beautiful dragon—who also was still one-hundred percent Shawna.

She lowered her head until we were more or less eye-to-eye. "I'm sorry I didn't tell you," she murmured, keeping her voice as soft as she could so as to not blow out my eardrums. "But I don't tell anybody. And I haven't shifted in—a long, long time.

I stared at her, my mind reeling. This explained many things, if I stopped and thought about it. Her vast wealth, of course, but I only just learned about that.

But also the way she'd count and recount her chips when we played poker, almost cooing over the stacks. The way when we traveled she loved to stack her suitcases and then sit on them. The way she never ever seemed to worry about any kind of physical danger—because of course she was never in physical danger. Very few things could take on a dragon—even one in human form.

Staring at her wings I thought, of course she was absolutely baffled in airports. She'd never needed to use planes to travel, at least until she—for some reason—decided to stop being a dragon.

I realized she was waiting for me to say something. "Of course I don't mind that you didn't tell me. But I'm so glad I know now. It's an awfully big thing to not know about a close friend."

I winced inwardly at "awfully big," but if she noticed the poor choice of words, I couldn't tell.

"I'm glad you know too," said Shawna with a relieved sigh that reeked of brimstone. "It'll sound weird, but I didn't think about being a dragon all that much. I mean, of course I did, but it's not like in every conversation we had I was thinking about it and not saying anything. I sort of—pushed it aside."

"But why?"

Shawna shook her head. "The short version is I had a falling out with my family. I will tell you the long version at some point, but not now. Now we have to get you to that concert."

I had all but forgotten about the concert and the rest of it, but at her words, it came back in a rush. Suddenly my adrenaline was pumping again.

"Okay, so, how does this work? Do I ride on your back, or do you carry me in your—talons—or something?"

Shawna chuckled. "No talons. I'll hunch down and it will be pretty easy to climb up on my back. There's a spot between my shoulders that's perfect for sitting. You'll see.

She hunkered down and I touched her side tentatively. She was hot to the touch. Not to the point where it would burn me, but hot. I was nervous enough that I might have chickened out, but I didn't want to hurt her feelings. And I desperately wanted to get back in time to see Mace.

To be honest I wasn't even certain what I was more nervous about, riding on Shawna's back or seeing Mace.

She was right, it was easy to climb up and soon I was sitting reasonably comfortably.

"Hold on tight to the spikes right in front of you," Shawna instructed over her shoulder. "My hide is so thick right there that I can't feel them really, so don't worry about hurting me."

I did as she said, then said "All set" in a voice that might have been too soft for her to hear with her human ears, but her dragon hearing was sharp.

"Then here we go!" She ran right off the roof of the building, her giant wings stretched out on either side, catching the air and causing us to glide along.

At first it was very peaceful, as she glided quietly over the town. But once we'd left the lights of the buildings and houses behind, she began flapping those monstrous wings and shit got a little scary.

The wind from the wings made me feel like I might be blown off her back at any moment. I was grateful she'd said I could hold on as tight as I liked. I was also grateful for the heat of her body. The higher we got the colder the air was, but it was like sitting on a radiator.

Finally she slowed into a glide again and called over her shoulder. "Nearly there!"

Far, far below, the lights of what I realized must be the festival shone brightly. Shawna circled, getting lower each time until we could make out the band on the stage.

"Listen," Shawna said over her shoulder, "this is how it's going to go down. I'm going to land behind that tent. It doesn't look like anyone's there right now. Jump off the moment I land, and I will shift instantly back into my human body. We will go around the tent and blend in with the crowd watching the show. Got it?"

"Got it," I yelled, hoping she'd hear me over the wind. I understood her precautions. Dragons garnered a lot of attention. It wasn't unheard of that one would fly to a concert, but it would draw a lot of gawkers. It's like driving up in a million-dollar car. You don't do it if you don't want everyone to notice you.

Shawna's plan worked perfectly, and soon we were merging with the hot, sweaty dancers right up by the stage. I'd never watched the band from this angle before.

I stared up at Mace, desperately wanting to touch him, but knowing I might never again. I was willing to take the risk of rejection for another chance. As I stared up at him, he looked right at me.

At least he seemed to—I was sure he couldn't make out anyone in the crowd. Or I was sure until I realized that Shawna was glowing, a sort of green-gold halo.

"Shawna," I hissed into her ear, "you're all lit up!"

"Crap, sorry. It sometimes happens after I shift back to human."

I was a bit surprised. My best friend in grade school had been a bear shifter, and while she might have shifted into bear form by accident if her emotions were heightened, her shifts back to human tended to be complete. She certainly never *glowed*.

That was the case with all the other shifters I knew, too. But maybe dragons were different. I looked back up at Mace but he wasn't looking our way anymore. He seemed a little happier, somehow, but that might have been my imagination. Good lord, I wanted to kiss him.

It occurred to me that this might be the last time I ever saw Mace up close. Not as close as I would have liked, but close enough to see how his eyes lit up when he sang, how his muscles rippled, how the sweat dripped off him.

I stared at him, drinking him in, trying to memorize every detail. I let his singing fill me, let the music into my body like I usually didn't dare. I'd already been moving because it was impossible not to, in that crowd, but now I began to let myself really dance, twisting and turning and jumping in a way I hadn't since college.

The music took me over and his voice enveloped me and my body wasn't entirely my own. I stared at Mace and allowed myself to love him, even though I knew it might be over, even though I was scared to death we wouldn't be able to work it out. I allowed myself to belong to him, one last time, to entirely be his.

I didn't want the set to ever end, I wanted to spend the rest of my life dancing and loving Mace. I knew heartbreak was waiting for me as soon as his singing stopped.

"Please," I thought, "let it never end."

They played for another hour, and I danced the entire time. I knew the set must be almost over when he turned and gestured to the rest of the band. They nodded and he turned back to the crowd. My heart sank. I wondered if I'd even get to say good-bye to him.

"Folks," Mace shouted into the mic, "we're going to end this show by doing something we swore we'd never do. But things can change just like that. Sometimes something happens, and it's like you're a new person. And folks, this new person is going to sing a gronk-blasted ballad."

There was a gasp from the crowd as the soft chords began. I was as shocked as anyone. Lots of Orc Rock bands did ballads, some every album, but AxeBender said they never would. But now they were.

As he began singing in a voice gentle and yet full of strength, I understood why, even though I still couldn't believe it. The song was about me. It didn't seem possible, and at first I thought I must be misunderstanding. But it was true.

I was pretty sure when he sang, "She's my friend and she's my lover, she's a witch and there's no other, she was here and now she's gone, I fucked it up, she said so long" but it was when he got to the hook that I couldn't deny it any longer.

Because he actually sang my name, over and over. "Alexis, Alexis please don't leave me, Alexis, Alexis, please believe me, I'd never do it, never be untrue, Alexis, Alexis, I love you."

My heart swelled and my head swam. It wasn't until cold air swirled around me that I even realized I was floating almost twenty feet in the air, eye level with Mace, above the crowd. We stared into each other's eyes as he sang the last few verses, and everything in the world melted away.

There was no crowd below me, no band behind him. The only thing that mattered was him and me and the love between us, the love that had lifted me into the air. I wanted to dance in front of him forever.

Finally, the last chord faded away and he dropped the mic. Mace reached towards me and I flew into his arms. As soon as they wrapped around me I knew, knew that betrayal had never been a possibility, and knew that forgiveness had never even been a question.

I belonged in his arms just as his arms belonged around me. We had known it the moment we'd met, however long it had taken us to admit it. We belonged to each other.

He held me for a long time, and then Torch came up and muttered that it was time for the next band to come on stage. I knew I should talk to the band, thank them for their help. I should find Shawna, too, let her know how grateful I was to her for knocking some sense into me. But all that would have to wait.

We ran off stage and into the nearest place away from everyone we could find—a shed built for holding landscaping equipment. The padlock melted away as we reached for the door.

As soon as we were inside he was kissing me, lifting me in the air, pressing me into the wall while his hands roughly tore off my dress. I wrapped my legs around him and the rest of our clothing dropped in tatters to the floor.

Our tongues invaded each other's mouths and our hands tangled in each other's hair and then he was entering me, pushing his way inside me with a new force and urgency. I jerked my hips against him and my body seemed to melt so that all that existed was his mouth on mine and his cock slamming inside me.

We rocked together and in no time at all my pussy was clenching and humming as I came, again and again. It was like his cock was stuffing orgasms into me. I came with each mighty thrust of him.

After an eternity of sweet nirvana, he swelled inside me and knew he was close. "Alexis," he groaned. "Alexis, I love you."

"I love you, Mace." Finally saying it out loud, confessing to him felt so good. As good as his cock in my pussy.

He thrust into me faster. "Tell me you're mine," he grunted. "Tell me you're mine forever."

"Forever," I agreed, feeling like my body was going to fly into a million pieces. "I'm yours Mace, forever and ever. I belong to you, I will always be yours."

He threw back his head and roared, a roar of pleasure and of love, and his cock throbbed and pulsed as he emptied load after load inside me. His seed was running down my legs, pooling on the floor, and still he came. It seemed like he would never stop coming and I came with him, writhing and shaking on that cock, screaming and panting.

Finally, we were spent and collapsed on the floor.

He cradled me in his arms and kissed my face. Then he rolled so I was on my back and he was on top of me. He gently nudged my knees apart and entered me again, this time slowly, tenderly, raining kisses on me as he moved in and out.

It felt like heaven, like pure joy, like pure love. I began to come again, but not violently like before. This filled my body like light, like honey melting into every inch of me.

He lowered his head to my ear, and whispered, "I love you Alexis. I love you, and I never want to kiss anyone but you, I never want to fuck anyone but you."

I was coming too hard to respond. I finally gasped out, "I love you, Mace, I'm so sorry I didn't trust you."

He pressed his lips to mine. "I promise you will never have to doubt me again."

He began to thrust a little faster, a little harder, and it was like going over a cliff, falling into an endless pit of ecstasy.

I lost all awareness of time, all awareness of anything but his body, and we stayed in that shed all night, moving together, making each other feel better than we'd ever felt before.

When we finally left, clad in the clothes I'd quickly and effortlessly repaired, the walk to the hotel seemed farther than we could bear. I counted windows and floors, figured out where my suite was, and took his hand. Flying was as easy as walking now, and a lot faster.

I flew him to the room and he ordered us room service, gulping down a Gatorade while I finally looked at my phone. Shawna had texted at some point in the night. The text simply said:

All good?

I thought for a moment, then texted in reply:

All very, very good.

Chapter Forty-Seven

MACE

She was mine. She was mine! She loved me as much as I loved her. That had never happened before with a girl, or at least it had never seemed like it. Aubrey was the worst, but with most of the girls I'd been with, we'd had uneven relationships. I was way more into Aubrey than she was into me, and the groupies were usually a lot more into me than I was with them.

But now, it was perfect. And I got to spend all my time with her, smelling her, feeling her, kissing her, talking with her, fucking her. She consumed me.

Of course there was also work. I was careful not to interfere when she had to concentrate on being a good manager. I talked about her respectfully when interviewed about the ballad, talked about how funny and smart she was and didn't mention how tight her pussy was or how it clenched my cock when I fucked her. "Her tits are so big and her pussy's so tight," would have been the quote of the year, but I managed to resist saying it out loud.

The band couldn't stop beaming at me until I told them I'd kick their asses if they didn't stop, which sparked the discussion we had at least once a month about who could kick whose ass. I was pretty sure I could take most of them, but they seemed sure I was wrong.

During the conversation, Alexis kept looking super amused and poking Shawna, who batted her hand away each time. What was *that* all about? But I didn't press them to find out.

Mostly because whenever I had Alexis alone I got distracted, either by fucking her or talking to her or kissing her or falling asleep with her in my arms. Or all of them at once. One time I woke up to discover I'd begun kissing her in my sleep while telling her how much I loved her, and she sat on my cock as soon as she was certain I was conscious.

She was my dream come true. My very own Alexis.

ALEXIS

The rest of the tour was like a dream. Now that pretty much everyone knew that Mace and I were together—the story of the ballad and all had made more than a few magazines—we didn't have to sneak around anymore. We were able to sleep in the same bed every night, sit on the bus together, doing crosswords and fucking whenever we thought no one would see.

I got some good-natured teasing from the record label, but it became really clear really fast that no one actually cared. Especially when the quality of my work didn't suffer. In fact, it got much, much better, because my new-found witchy powers meant I was a thousand times more organized than before. Not knowing where to find a file or piece of information? Not a problem. I concentrated for a moment and *poof* it appeared before me.

I thought about whether to tell my family about how strong my powers had become, and finally decided to wait until my next visit. I was going to bring Mace to meet them, and the shock of my dating a rock star would surely undercut their smug pleasure at my finally doing like they always wanted, being a powerful witch who would make the family look good.

Normally when the tour ended it would have meant me going on to a different tour with a different band. But the record label and the band suggested I manage the band full-time.

I'd always wanted to be a tour manager, traveling three hundred days of the year, but now settling down in one spot for a little while seemed like a good idea. It wouldn't be too much time in one place—the band would break for a couple months, then go into the studio to record a new album, do a short three-month tour, take another short break, and then do a major tour when the new album came out.

It was a tighter schedule than a lot of bands followed, but as Clash explained it, "AxeBender likes making new music. AxeBender likes touring. AxeBender likes money." Clash didn't usually talk about the band in the third person like that, but he was exceptionally drunk. Or, as he kept explaining it, "Clash had too much orc-ahol." It made all the groupies in the room laugh. We laughed too, but later, and we were laughing *at* him not with him.

As the tour wound down, we made our plans. Mace had a very nice apartment, plenty big enough for the two of us, and it didn't take much persuading to convince me to move in. It was near both the studio and their rehearsal space, and all his bandmates were in the same building. When I gently suggested that maybe that was weird, they looked at me blankly.

"If we didn't live right next to each other, we wouldn't get to hang out every day," Jax explained.

"Well, we would," Frey put in, "but it would be a pain. This way we can walk up or down the stairs to see each other."

So, living with Mace meant having all his bandmates in my life pretty much full-time, too. It was a good thing I liked them all so much. And Mace promised plenty of vacations to tropical paradises where we could fuck on the beach all day long.

The last night of the tour, I watched him from the side stage. Often, now, I was in the audience for shows, dancing in front of the stage. But this time I wanted to watch him the way I had that very first night. To see his passion for his music, his glistening body, how when he sang he managed to look both incredibly dangerous and incredibly safe. I danced to the music several feet above the floor, feeling the music take me the same way he took me, every chance he got.

I'd finally found the man who could fill not just my pussy but my heart and mind. He fulfilled me. He showed me what I wanted my life to be. He was my very own Mace.

The only thing I didn't talk to Mace about was Shawna. I mean, obviously we talked about Shawna—she was my best friend. But I didn't tell Mace that she was a dragon. I would never keep my own secrets from him, but that wasn't my secret to tell. I figured it would come out soon enough, and I was right.

Chapter Forty-Eight: Epilogue

ALEXIS

The morning after the last show of the tour, we all went down to the hotel restaurant together. It was like the first time the seven of us had eaten breakfast together, except that now I was able to sit next to Mace and touch his arm and smile at him as much as I liked.

I even fed him a little until the others demanded we stop it. We also got way better food and service. The others didn't seem to notice, but everyone working at the hotel knew that Shawna was their ultimate boss.

I didn't notice when the elf first walked into the room. But Shawna gasped and turned pale as she stared at something behind me. I twisted around as a tall, thin man dressed in gold and green livery made his regal way towards our table.

He walked directly to Shawna and bowed low. After a moment, he straightened and held out a gold envelope. She tucked her hands behind her, but he didn't move, didn't even blink. He stood there holding the envelope out to her. Finally, she took it from him, and he turned and walked silently away.

We all stared at Shawna as she stared at the envelope. She looked like she wanted to throw it away, but she didn't have the chance—it jerked in her hand and the flap opened.

A stream of red paper hearts flew out and floated in the air, followed by two paper-thin cupids, spinning and dancing and winking at us while blowing little trumpets. A piece of gold paper came next. There was black text on the paper, in such intricate calligraphy that it was unreadable (to me anyway) but that was okay, as an angelic voice came from nowhere and read the page aloud.

"Miss Sh'wannder'fin Withern," the voice intoned, "Fr'soran'ter Withern and R'bek'tra Withern have the pleasure of requesting your presence at the wedding of Kl'yana'fin Withern and G'geor'juun Craw in two weeks' time, at the Withern ancestral estate."

Shawna made a strangled sound, like she was trying not to scream or puke. The paper folded itself neatly and dropped to the table in front of her, as did the hearts and cupids. I thought it was done, but then the envelope wriggled one more time and a flat origami dragon slid onto the table.

It puffed itself out and flew in loop-de-loops over our heads, then shot out the window. I assumed to inform the sender that the invitation had been successfully received.

Shawna sat frozen. We all stared at her. She eventually noticed and seemed to realize we were all wondering what the hell had happened.

She swallowed hard before speaking. "I'm really sorry," she said, finally. "I'm so sorry."

There was a pause. I didn't know what I could say that wouldn't reveal secrets she still might not be ready to reveal. At last Torch spoke up. "You're forgiven. Sorry for what?"

Shawna's eyes found mine, and I smiled reassuringly. I tried to silently assure her that it was okay to tell or okay not to, whatever she preferred.

She looked at the invitation lying in front of her and a single tear fell and splashed on the envelope.

When she spoke, her voice was a little raspy. "Okay, look, I really like you guys, okay? So I'm going to tell you some stuff." We all nodded. And then it came out in a rush. "Well, first off, Alexis already knows this part, I'm a shapeshifter. A dragon shapeshifter."

There was the expected chorus of "whoa"s and "cool"s and "wait, what?"s. Shawna ignored it.

"My whole family is dragons. They're sort of an old dragon family, and, well, you probably already know that dragons are super rich and formal, and that's how I grew up. My real name is Sh'wannder'fin. I go by Shawna for short."

"A couple of years ago I had a big falling out with my family and I sort of disappeared off the map, and didn't tell anyone I was a shapeshifter. My family bugged me a lot at first but eventually left me alone when I said I'd make a public fuss. Left me alone until a few weeks ago when I turned into a dragon for the first time in, like, years."

"No way were they going to let me fly around and make a spectacle of myself as an independent dragon. Oh no. But they couldn't come out and say that, they had to be as passive aggressive as they always are. The very next day I got a stupid note from my stupid mother saying she was so glad I had decided to return to the family. I sent back a note that said, "NOT," but clearly they didn't pay attention."

She paused to sniff. Torch, who was sitting next to her, put his arm around her. He was such a good guy. I was grateful to him. I wanted to do the same but I was on the other side of the table, pushed against the wall.

Shawna leaned against Torch and sighed. "And now they've sent me *this*." She looked at the wedding invitation with a loathing that would maybe be fitting for a slug slime smoothie. The hatred on her face was intense.

"Of course I'm certain, we're all certain, that you have a good reason for hating your family, but why do you hate the wedding invitation so much?" I asked, as gently as I could.

For a moment I thought Shawna wasn't going to answer, then she looked up at us, nostrils flared and eyes blazing. She looked exactly like a dragon in human form, and thin trails of smoke came out of her nostrils. Scales rippled faintly across her fingers and I hoped she wasn't going to shift right there at the table. There wasn't room.

"I was invited," she said in a voice that was terrifyingly calm, "to the wedding of my sister and her fiancé." We all glanced at one another, still confused. "And the icing on the cake is that they used the exact wedding invitation he and I used, back when he was *my* fiancé. Which he was, right up until I had the bad fortune to walk in on him fucking my sister."

There was a long silence and then the table exploded.

"You've got to be fucking kidding me," Mace said.

"What the actual FUCK?" Frey spat.

Jax and Clash just said fuck, a lot.

"Oh Shawna, oh no Shawna," I said over and over again, like an idiot. I didn't know what else to say. I was so sorry and angry. I clenched my hands around my fork so hard they hurt.

Torch didn't say anything, just tightened his arm around her.

Shawna smiled weakly at us and then started to cry as she said, "And now I have to go to their goddamned wedding, because the only thing more humiliating than going would be not going and having everyone laugh at me for being too scared to show. Or having my mother come and collect me and force me to go."

Frey and I both started to protest, but she shook her head, hard.

"Trust me," she said. "There's no way. Now that they know that I know about the wedding, I have to be there. I have to hold my head high and go."

She started to sob, and Torch took her fully into his arms. "It's okay," he said, and, to my surprise, kissed her hair. "It's not like you're going alone."

THE END.

Thank you for reading about Alexis and Mace! To find out what happens with Torch and Shawna join Flora's mailing list or like Flora on Facebook.

About Authors

Flora Dare lives in Durham, NC in a cute little pink house, with her husband, Scott, their kiddo, and their hellion of a puppy, HaliToeses. She writes love, lust, and mayhem in almost every flavor, and like The Pirate Movie, she wants a happy ending, every time!

Josie Kell lives in Washington, DC, where she likes to go on long walks with her husband, read aloud to her many dogs, and go to rock concerts. If you ask her what her favorite book is, she'll stare at you in horror before demanding you specify a sub-sub-sub-sub-genre.

ALSO BY FLORA DARE

A Fated Mate for the Pack Boss

Wolf shifter Lili Thornhill hides beneath ugly clothes and sensible shoes, but the yearning in her heart is for a mate and a family. As a low ranking member of her pack, Lili barely dares to dream about a fated mate, let alone her boss and Alpha, Cole Burnett. Cole is new to the role of Alpha and is under a lot of pressure to pick a high-ranking wolf as a mate,to help settle the pack. He never looks twice at his dowdy admin, Lili.

Until one day when Cole stumbles on Lili skinny dipping and his eyes are opened to just how beautiful she is. Can Cole keep Lili safe from a pack who would rather see her dead than in their alpha's arms?

Mate in a Minute Box Set

The Mate in a Minute series of sexy short stories deliver a happy ending right before bed. You're welcome ;)

Badgering the Bear

Curvy badger shifter Jolie is nagged by her best friend to check out shifter speed dating (okay, she might have lost a bet). It's pretty boring, though, until she sees...him. Gabe is big. He's burly. And just the touch of his hand on hers sets Jolie's body aflame with need.

Insecurity sends Jolie scurrying for the cover of the forest. Good thing a bear like Gabe loves a good hunt. And what Gabe wants? Gabe takes.

Charming the Wolf

After losing a bet with her bestie, fox shifter Zanea 'Zane' Russell must endure a night of speed dating all the local rabbits, hounds and squirrels. Not exactly the recipe for getting swept off her feet...until HE sits down across from her.

Wolf shifter Josh Landry agrees to one night of speed dating to get his nagging brothers off his back. Little do they know that he's not going to accept or ask for any dates. Even if they're curvy, foxy bombshells who make every part of him tingle.

But when Zane gets her list of date requests the next day, Josh isn't on it...

Taming the Lion

Everyone around her is finding mates and bear shifter Desdemona "Des" Jacobs is determined not to be left behind. Despite a bad breakup, she decides to try her hand at speed dating.

Lion shifter Drake Sheridan let Des go when they were young. He knows it was a mistake and hopes that they can have a second chance at a mating. When he sees her at the speed dating event, he thinks it's fate bringing them together.

But Des can't date Drake with a clear heart. Her terrifying ex is still stalking her, and she's afraid of him getting hurt. Can she even think of a happy ever after with the man she's always wanted when the past won't let her go?

Made in the USA
Coppell, TX
07 June 2022